The Inn at Holiday Bay:
Letters in the Library

by

Kathi Daley

I want to thank the very talented Jessica Fischer for the cover art.

I so appreciate Bruce Curran, who is always ready and willing to answer my cyber questions; Jayme Maness for helping out with the book clubs; and Peggy Hyndman for helping sleuth out those pesky typos.

And, of course, thanks to the readers and bloggers in my life, who make doing what I do possible.

Thank you to Randy Ladenheim-Gil for the editing.

And finally, I want to thank my husband Ken for allowing me time to write by taking care of everything else.

Books by Kathi Daley
Come for the murder, stay for the romance.

Zoe Donovan Cozy Mystery:

Halloween Hijinks
The Trouble With Turkeys
Christmas Crazy
Cupid's Curse
Big Bunny Bump-off
Beach Blanket Barbie
Maui Madness
Derby Divas
Haunted Hamlet
Turkeys, Tuxes, and Tabbies
Christmas Cozy
Alaskan Alliance
Matrimony Meltdown
Soul Surrender
Heavenly Honeymoon
Hopscotch Homicide
Ghostly Graveyard
Santa Sleuth
Shamrock Shenanigans
Kitten Kaboodle
Costume Catastrophe
Candy Cane Caper
Holiday Hangover
Easter Escapade
Camp Carter

Trick or Treason
Reindeer Roundup
Hippity Hoppity Homicide
Firework Fiasco
Henderson House
Holiday Hostage
Lunacy Lake – *Summer 2019*

Zimmerman Academy The New Normal
Zimmerman Academy New Beginnings
Ashton Falls Cozy Cookbook

Tj Jensen Paradise Lake Mysteries by Henery Press:

Pumpkins in Paradise
Snowmen in Paradise
Bikinis in Paradise
Christmas in Paradise
Puppies in Paradise
Halloween in Paradise
Treasure in Paradise
Fireworks in Paradise
Beaches in Paradise
Thanksgiving in Paradise – *Fall 2019*

Whales and Tails Cozy Mystery:

Romeow and Juliet
The Mad Catter

Grimm's Furry Tail
Much Ado About Felines
Legend of Tabby Hollow
Cat of Christmas Past
A Tale of Two Tabbies
The Great Catsby
Count Catula
The Cat of Christmas Present
A Winter's Tail
The Taming of the Tabby
Frankencat
The Cat of Christmas Future
Farewell to Felines
A Whisker in Time
The Catsgiving Feast
A Whale of a Tail – *Spring 2019*

Writers' Retreat Southern Seashore Mystery:

First Case
Second Look
Third Strike
Fourth Victim
Fifth Night
Sixth Cabin
Seventh Chapter
Eighth Witness

Rescue Alaska Paranormal Mystery:

Finding Justice
Finding Answers
Finding Courage
Finding Christmas
Finding Shelter – *Spring 2019*

A Tess and Tilly Mystery:

The Christmas Letter
The Valentine Mystery
The Mother's Day Mishap
The Halloween House
The Thanksgiving Trip
The Saint Paddy's Promise – *March 2019*

The Inn at Holiday Bay:

Boxes in the Basement
Letters in the Library
Message in the Mantel – *Spring 2019*

Family Ties:

The Hathaway Sisters
Harper – *February 2019*
Harlow – *Spring 2019*

Haunting by the Sea:

Homecoming by the Sea
Secrets by the Sea
Missing by the Sea
Betrayal by the Sea – *March 2019*

Sand and Sea Hawaiian Mystery:

Murder at Dolphin Bay
Murder at Sunrise Beach
Murder at the Witching Hour
Murder at Christmas
Murder at Turtle Cove
Murder at Water's Edge
Murder at Midnight

Seacliff High Mystery:

The Secret
The Curse
The Relic
The Conspiracy
The Grudge
The Shadow
The Haunting

Road to Christmas Romance:

Road to Christmas Past

Chapter 1

If there is anything I have learned over the course of the past fourteen months, it is that life is fluid and evolving. It is made up of highs and lows that seem to merge one into the other as events unfold and memories take us where they might. It is messy and unpredictable, and a single unforeseen moment can result in an event so unimaginable, it can cast us into our own personal hell. But life can also surprise and uplift us. It can bring joy and laughter, and if we open ourselves to its presence, it can bring a breathless beauty mere words cannot convey. Life can energize and enrich us, it can provide meaning and belonging in places never expected. Life is a state into which we are born, but in the course of living out our moments, it can also be a decision we are challenged to make.

Fourteen months ago, my husband Ben and infant son Johnathan were killed in a senseless accident that sent me into the darkest depths of despair. At the time, it seemed easier to give in, to lose myself in the darkness, but somewhere along the way, I'd found a reason to choose life, and with that choice, a willingness to dig myself out of my grief one painful moment at a time.

Today would have been Ben's thirty-fifth birthday had he lived, which, if it had been anything like his thirtieth birthday, would most likely have resulted in a day of sullen introspection on his part. Ben had serious goals for his life, and a timeline marked off in five-year increments that corresponded to those goals. If his timeline was off by even a tiny bit when a defining birthday came around, you could bet that champagne toasts and decadent cakes would have been replaced by the sort of despondent torment that would make him almost unbearable to be around. Of course, in this moment, as I sat in a dark room and remembered my life with the man I had loved with my whole being, I knew in my heart I would welcome despondent torment, or really any mood, if it meant that Ben and I could be together even one more day.

God, I missed him.

I leaned back into the pillows I'd stacked against my headboard as a deep sorrow engulfed me. Rufus, the cat I'd never wanted but now couldn't imagine living without, snuggled up next to me, purring loudly. I leaned over and turned on the bedside lamp. Opening the drawer of the nightstand, I pulled out a small box. Taking a deep breath, I lifted the lid, then reached into the box and pulled out a photo. The one I'd randomly chosen had been taken of Ben the day he'd made detective. I ran a finger over his huge grin. He'd been so happy and proud. He'd worked hard and never looked back despite the challenges he'd been tasked with along the way. Ben had most definitely been a disciplined fellow, and with the promotion, he'd actually been ahead of his schedule, so maybe this birthday, unlike his thirtieth, would have been all smiles and happy celebration.

Rufus butted his head under my chin, in a move I'd come to recognize as his attempt to offer comfort when I was sad. I scratched him behind the ears, then picked up another photo of Ben and me on our wedding day. A single tear trailed down my cheek as I turned the photo over to find our names, Ben and Abby Sullivan, along with the date of our union, and the location, in the heart of San Francisco, where we'd promised to love and honor each other until death do us part.

Until death do us part. Who could have guessed that death would part us a mere five years after we pledged our lives to each other?

I replaced the photo and rummaged through the box, which also contained photos of the first little apartment we lived in before we were even married, my first book signing, the trip to Mexico we took when I made the *New York Times* Bestsellers list, and, of course, many, many photos of the unexpected and unplanned but very welcome child who had come from our union. Ben loved Johnathan and would have been a good father, but I did have to wonder how a baby in the house might have altered the life path he had set up for himself. Would he have taken changes to that plan with a grain of salt or would he have eventually sunk into a depression he might never have been able to work himself out of? Now I guess we'd never know.

Johnathan had only been five weeks old when a distracted driver had swerved into Ben's lane, ripping both my husband and my infant son from my life. Ben had never wanted children, and to be honest, prior to having Johnathan, a baby was the farthest thing from my mind as well. But once Johnathan was born, and I'd held him in my arms, I knew that he occupied a hole in my life that could never have been filled by anyone as completely as it had been by the tiny little gift from heaven that had arrived two weeks early on a rainy fall day.

I set the box of photos on the nightstand and glanced out the window. It was early. Still dark. I doubted that my roommate would be up, which was just as well because I felt that I needed some time to pull my ragged emotions into line. After Ben and Johnathan died, I hadn't wanted to go on living. I was so lost and afraid. I truly believed my life was over, and I hadn't known what to do to find my way back to the living. Those first weeks of empty rooms, pitying glances, and days without hope of happiness were the darkest of my life. But then I'd seen an ad for a dilapidated old mansion perched high upon a bluff overlooking the sea, and I knew that if I ever wanted to reenter the land of the living, I'd need a fresh start and a new perspective. I paid cash for the house sight unseen, packed up my belongings, and moved from San Francisco, California, to Holiday Bay, Maine, where I found the new life I'd longed for and a reason to go on.

Making a decision, I slid my legs out of bed and sat up. It had been a while since I'd taken Rufus to Velma's Café for his favorite meal of scrambled eggs. Velma was one of the first people I'd met after arriving in Holiday Bay and I still considered her to be one of the most important people in my East Coast life, second only to my new best friend and roommate, Georgia Carter, who had shown up on my doorstep a couple of months ago with her huge black dog, Ramos. Since Velma and Georgia had become a daily part of my life, the world had opened up for me, and things I'd once thought impossible had begun to fall into place. Getting out of bed, I slipped on a pair of jeans, a long-sleeved T-shirt, and a heavy sweatshirt, then padded into the bathroom to brush my teeth and comb my hair. Tiptoeing so as not to wake Georgia, I picked up Rufus and headed out into the frigid morning.

I paused after exiting the cottage and looked out toward the sea. The dawn of a new day was just beginning to light the horizon. It was a frosty morning and I'd heard they were predicting snow, but in this isolated moment, as I looked toward the distant light, I felt a deep gratitude for the life I had discovered. From the moment I'd first seen the cottage on the rocky bluff overlooking the sea, I knew in my heart that fate had led me to the exact spot in time and space where I needed to be to rebuild my shattered life.

******

The lull between the enchantment and magic of the Christmas Festival and the elegance and romance of the Valentine's Ball had settled over Holiday Bay, bringing a quiet I found welcoming. Not that I hadn't enjoyed the festival, which ran from the day after Thanksgiving until Christmas Eve, but I found that after the energy of the holiday season, I longed for the quiet and serenity that comes with a slower pace. Of course, I supposed that at least part of my appreciation for the silence stemmed from the fact that I was smack dab in the middle of the remodel on the mansion and my days at home tended to be loud, and crowded, and hectic. A lot more hectic, I realized, than I had ever imagined they would be.

"Morning, Velma," I said to the woman I'd met on my first morning in Holiday Bay and now called a friend.

"Abby; Rufus. It's been a while since the two of you have been in."

I hung up my jacket and then slipped into a booth. The diner was deserted so early in the morning, which was just fine with me. "I've been busy with the remodel, as well as the novel, so I have been staying close to home. Rufus and I woke up early this morning and decided it was a good day to come in and say hi."

Velma set a menu on the table. "Georgia not with you?"

"Georgia and Ramos were still sleeping when we left the cottage."

"Well, I'm glad the two of you stopped by. It's been quiet now that the holiday is over. What can I get for you?"

"I'll have biscuits and sausage gravy and Rufus will have scrambled eggs."

Velma set a cup of coffee in front of me, then hurried off to make our meals. Rufus, who was familiar with the procedure, followed Velma into the kitchen, where he would eat in the mudroom at the back of the building. Once they had disappeared from sight, I took out my phone and checked my messages. There was one from my agent, asking for an update on the manuscript I was working on, one from an old friend of Ben's, acknowledging his birthday and wishing me all the best on what must be a difficult day, and one from my insurance agent, asking for some additional information for my homeowner's policy. The most surprising message of all, however, was a short email from my sister, Annie, letting me know that she was thinking of me today.

As I read the email for a second time, I put my hand over my heart and sucked in a deep breath. Tears I had been valiantly holding at bay streamed down my cheeks as I pictured my sister in my mind. In the months since I'd left California for Maine, I'd longed for even a small glimmer of hope that my relationship with Annie could be repaired, and after months without a word from her, this was the first time I actually felt hope.

"What is it?" Velma asked, setting a plate of food in front of me.

I used the back of my hand to wipe the moisture from my face. "It's nothing. I'm fine."

"My eyesight might not be as good as it once was, but you don't look fine." Velma sat across from me. She placed her hand on my forearm. "What is it, sugar? Maybe I can help."

I took a deep breath and let it out slowly. "Today would have been Ben's birthday."

"Ah. I see. I guess that events such as birthdays never celebrated would lend themselves to a few tears." Velma handed me a napkin. "You go ahead and have yourself a good cry."

I took the napkin from Velma and wiped my eyes. "I know this is going to sound crazy, but I've already spent some time this morning with my memories of Ben, and I think I am going to be okay. The fact that it would have been his thirty-fifth birthday, which admittedly is a big one, isn't really responsible for these tears."

"So what is behind those leaky eyes?"

"I received an email from my sister, Annie."

"Sister?' Velma raised a brow. "I didn't know you had a sister. You've never mentioned her."

I took a sip of my coffee and leaned back in the booth. "We've been estranged ever since I made the decision to move to Holiday Bay. At least we've been estranged on her part. It's sort of confusing, but basically, I was such a mess after Ben died, and Annie tried to help me through it. The problem was, at the time I didn't want to get through it and wasn't ready to let go of my grief, so I guess I pushed her away. She still hung by me despite my sour mood, until I decided to use my share of the money our grandmother left us to buy the house here. She thought I was making a terrible and impulsive mistake and tried to stop me from both buying the house and making the move. When I chose to ignore her pleas, she tried to stop me legally, and when that didn't work, she removed herself from the situation and hasn't spoken to or even communicated with me since."

"Oh darling, I'm so sorry. To lose a sister after having lost so much. I just can't imagine."

"It's been tough, and I have been trying to find a way back to her. Ever since I've been living in Holiday Bay, I've been writing her chatty emails about the house and the town, hoping that she would see that I was happy. I hoped if she could see that, and the decision to move here wasn't a huge mistake, she would choose to let bygones be bygones and be happy with me. But until today, she hadn't responded to any of the dozens of emails I've sent."

"And today?" Velma asked.

"She sent me just a single sentence that let me know she was thinking of me. It's not a lot, but it is something. To me, the act offers hope that maybe at some point in the future we can heal our relationship. She's the only family I have left." I glanced at Velma. "Well, at least the only family that is related by blood. Since moving to Holiday Bay, I feel like I have a new family that means much more to me than I can ever say."

"I know what you mean. One of the reasons I would never consider a move from Holiday Bay is because I have family here, although truth be told, not a single member of that family is related by blood."

"Your parents are no longer with you?"

Velma shook her head. "They've been gone a long time. I do, like you, have a sister, but like you, we are estranged. She moved away a very long time ago and I haven't seen her since."

"I'm so sorry. When was the last time you saw your sister?"

"More than thirty years ago."

I choked on my coffee. "Thirty years? But why? It seems that in thirty years you could have found a way to mend fences."

Velma shrugged. "The years get away from you if you aren't keeping a close eye on them. When Regina left, I assumed she'd be back. I really didn't even fret about her departure at the time. We had both set our sights on the same guy, a guy she loved but who chose me, and I guess I figured that a little separation would be good for us. I hoped it would give us some perspective so that we could talk things through and put our argument behind us." A look of sadness came over Velma's face. "I really thought she'd be home by Christmas. Reggie loved Christmas at Holiday Bay. But Christmas came and went and she didn't come home, so I decided to set my sights on the following December. But the years sort of melted one into the other, and she never did come home. I guess at this point I should assume she never will."

"And the guy?"

"Married him." Velma let out a laugh that sounded more like a snort. "Didn't last more than a couple of miserable years. Guess I should have let Reggie have him, but I was young and he was everything I thought I'd ever wanted. He was a mistake I have lived to regret."

"You should go to Reggie and talk to her. Tell her that you made a mistake and are sorry."

"Can't. I have no idea where she is."

"There must be a way to find her. Have you tried?"

Velma shook her head. "Seems pointless at this point in time. I may not have known where to find Reggie all these years, but she knew where to find me. If she had wanted to talk to me at any point during the past thirty years, she could have called or come by." Velma looked up as a family of six came in through the front door. "I need to get to work. You enjoy those biscuits."

That family turned out to be the beginning of the breakfast crowd, so I finished my food in silence. Wow, thirty years. I guess I understood how little things could turn into big things and people we cared about could drift away, but thirty years? Maybe

Velma didn't know where her sister was after all this time, but the mystery writer in me assured me that there must be a way to find her. With today's technology, oftentimes a name and a directed internet search was enough to provide the information I knew we'd need to at least begin our search.

Velma was still busy when I'd finished my meal, so it seemed apparent I wouldn't be able to speak to her about it today. I left a nice tip, grabbed Rufus, and headed to my car. As long as I was in town, I figured I'd stop by the market, so I set Rufus on the passenger seat of my SUV and drove in that direction. The town was beginning to show signs of life by this point, as folks headed to work and parents began ferrying their children to school.

After I purchased the items I needed, I headed out to the parking lot, where I stood for a moment and simply listened to the sound of the wind whistling through the trees. Snow flurries filled the air, blocking out the clear skies I'd woken to. Winter in Maine certainly wasn't for everyone, with the frigid temperatures and frequent snow, but given the current parameters of my life, I actually found the isolation to be pretty perfect.

Once my groceries were loaded, I returned the store cart and headed home. *Home*, I thought to myself. A word that means so much more than just a place to hang one's hat. A word that at one point in my life I'd taken for granted. A word I'd lost along the way, only to rediscover it in a place I'd never imagined before tragedy had consumed my life.

Chapter 2

"Lonnie was by earlier," Georgia said as soon as I walked into the oceanfront cottage we shared with an armful of groceries. "He said that there is a situation with the plumbing and he'd like you to stop over at the house when you have a chance."

I set the brown paper bags on the counter and then brushed the snow from my long dark hair. "Did he say what the problem with the plumbing entailed?"

"No." Georgia shook her head, her long blond braid swaying with her movement. "He just said he needed to speak to you. He had a man with him. I can't be certain who he was, but from the clothes he was wearing, I assume he must have been the plumber."

"Okay. I'll head over there now. I couldn't find the brand of white chocolate you asked for, but the man at the store said this one would work just as well."

"I'm sure it will be fine. And thank you. I might have overcommitted just a bit when I volunteered to provide all the sweets for the bake sale the children's art project is holding this weekend."

I smiled but didn't respond. Georgia was a genius in the kitchen, and her baked goods already had potential customers from miles around talking about the inn and the food that they anticipated would be found there. If I had to guess, we were going to be sold out the first six months we were in business. "I'm going to run over to talk to Lonnie before I get busy and forget all about it. When I get back we can go over the formatting for the new website. I have everything set up so all we have to do is preview it, make sure it appears the way we want it to, and then we can go live."

Georgia's blue eyes shone with excitement. "I can't believe how fast we got that together. Once we get the website up, folks should start talking about our theme weekends, wine tastings, and special events. I have a feeling we are going to have folks clamoring to make reservations."

"I was just thinking the same thing."

"I don't suppose Lonnie has said exactly when we might be able to open?"

"When we first got started, he said July," I answered. "I'll ask him if he is still on track now that he has had a chance to really dig into things. The first floor seemed to go pretty fast, but there is a lot more heavy-duty renovation to be done on the second and third floors."

Georgia paused with a sack of flour in her hands. "It'd be fun to open for the Fourth of July, but I don't want to book anything that close to our anticipated opening date in the event that problems pop up along the way. I think for now we should just take the names and email addresses of anyone who's interested in booking with us and we can get back to them when we have a firm date."

"I totally agree. It would be too stressful to have people booked and then not be able to open on time for one reason or another."

"As soon as we start to gather some email addresses, we might want to send out a newsletter with updates on the renovation."

"I love the idea of a newsletter. I would think there would be a fair number of people who would be interested in the renovation process. And a newsletter would be a good way to keep our potential guests engaged until we are far enough along to begin taking bookings." I paused to let the idea settle. "You know, even once the construction is complete, we are going to have a lot of work to do to get the place ready. We'll need to buy furniture, dishware, and linens. We may even want to think about a fall opening."

"Just in time for leaf-changing season," Georgia said. "I am anxious to get started, but I suppose a fall opening would be less stressful than trying to open for the summer season. If we can set a firm date, we might even be able to book the rooms clear through until the end of the year. Maybe we can have a huge open house on Labor Day weekend."

"That might be something to consider."

I watched as Rufus sauntered up to Georgia's dog, Ramos, and then headed back out the door. I could hear Van Halen blasting from someone's radio before I reached the main house, where the men and women on Lonnie's crew were hammering and sawing and singing along to the loud rock and roll music.

When I entered the house through the new French doors that made up an entire wall of the dining area, I paused to look around. Things really were coming together. When I'd first arrived at the dilapidated old house two months ago, I have to admit that I suffered more than a few moments of panic as I realized the enormity of the project I'd taken on. But then I met Lonnie Parker, and his confident approach to the remodel, as well as his love for every step of the project, helped me to overcome my fear and embrace the magic of the whole thing.

"Oh good, you are here," Lonnie said as he walked up with a tall man who looked to be in his fifties, carrying a clipboard. "Abby Sullivan, this is Lucas Fitzgerald. Lucas owns Fitzgerald Plumbing. It seems we may have a small problem with the bathroom addition we are doing on the first floor."

"I'm happy to meet you, ma'am," Lucas said.

"Likewise." I smiled back at him. "I thought the first-floor bath was already done."

"Everything has been installed and is ready to go, but I had Lucas come by to hook things up, and he noticed a problem I didn't."

"What seems to be the problem?"

"Water pressure and old pipes," the plumber replied.

"I'm afraid I'll need more than that," I said in response.

"There are actually two separate but related problems," Lonnie informed me. "The first is that the old pipes that fed the small bath we tore out to build the pantry are too narrow to accommodate the water flow capacity necessary for the new features we decided to add to the bathrooms, including the

Jacuzzi tub, the rain shower, and the double sinks. If we want to upgrade the fixtures, we are going to need to upgrade the pipes."

"And the second problem?" I asked. "You said there were two."

"The water heater that is located downstairs and services the kitchen, laundry, and guest bath, is pretty far away from the new bath we are building as part of the suite. I'd planned to run new pipes under the floor and splice into the existing system, but Lucas here thinks it makes more sense if we tap into the new water heater we are installing on the second floor, which will be located just above the new bathroom. To do that, we will need to tear into the wall in the library, which is next to the utility closet, and replace the pipes. That would be a relatively easy solution except for the fact that we will need to remove and replace the preexisting shelving in the library, which we had talked about trying to preserve."

I looked at Lucas. "Will going up through the wall be less expensive than running new pipes to service the bathroom?"

"A lot less expensive," Lucas confirmed. "Plus your guests won't be competing for hot water with the laundry and dishwasher."

I looked at Lonnie. "Okay. Then go ahead and take out the wall. I've been thinking about replacing the bookshelves with the same wood we plan to use in the third-floor parlor. I think in the long run it will provide more cohesion between the rooms."

Lonnie blew out a breath that I imagined was a sigh of relief. "I couldn't agree more. I think that it will cost a bit more, but we can repurpose the wood from the old bookshelves for other rooms. In the long run, I think new shelving in the library will look fabulous."

I looked at Lucas. "I would like to see a full estimate for the additional work we have just discussed before you order supplies or start the demo. You can just give it to Lonnie."

"Yes, ma'am. I'll get to work on that right away."

After Lucas left I looked at Lonnie. "What was with the ma'am? Do I look that old today?"

Lonnie laughed. "You look beautiful today, as always. Lucas is an old-fashioned sort who calls any women he doesn't know well ma'am, especially when he meets them for the first time in an official capacity. Once he gets to know you a bit, I'm sure he'll refer to you as Abby."

"I hope so. I don't think I'm quite ready to be called ma'am. So, how are things going overall? Are we still on track to be done in June or July?"

"June no, July maybe. The first floor should be done by the end of this month with the exception of the refurbishment of the mantel. It is such an old and intricately carved piece, and I know you said you wanted to preserve it, so I thought I'd call in a buddy of mine who specializes in repairing and refurbishing old wood. He's a real artist. I think you will really be happy with his work."

"Do you think he might be able to replicate the crown molding that is missing in the dining room?"

"Actually, I do. If anyone can, Bobby can. He is booked up through the end of the month, but he said he could get us on his calendar for late February if we are interested."

"If you think he is our guy, book him. I'd love to have the first floor done. I think the place will begin to feel more like a home once I can begin to decorate and fill the place with furniture."

"You might want to hold off on that until we finish the demo on the second and third floors. It'll be dusty, that's for sure, and I'd hate to see you move in furniture that could end up being damaged."

"You make a good point." I clasped my hands together. "I'm just getting so excited to get things underway."

"I will say that you and Georgia have done a good job spreading the hype. Folks around town are already talking about your ideas for destination weddings, theme weekends, and outdoor concerts on the bluff. I think this place is going to be huge. A real must-see venue on the New England coastline."

"I hope so." I glanced at my watch. "I should get back. I arranged to call my agent this afternoon, and I want to have everything together that I know she will ask me about."

"Before you go, Lacy wanted me to invite you and Georgia to dinner this Saturday. It is the twins' birthday and we are going to have a few friends join us for the celebration."

"I'd love to come. I'll ask Georgia and then call Lacy to confirm."

"That'd be great. Lacy has told me time and time again how much she enjoys spending time with you and Georgia. She said she'd been so busy being a wife and mother that she had almost forgotten what it was like to be a friend."

I laughed. "I have to say that she has been good for me as well. Your woman knows how to have a good time. The last time she took Georgia and me antiquing and wine tasting, I think I laughed more than I ever have in my whole life."

"Lacy is good that way. She knows how to squeeze the most out of life. That is one of the main reasons I fell in love with her. Well, that and her lasagna. The woman can cook."

I nodded. "Yes, she can."

By the time I got back to the cottage, Georgia had put away the groceries and started browning sausage for the pasta dish she was making for dinner. "I need to do some work before I call Kate and I told her I'd call her at five, so I'll be in my room."

"What time would you like dinner to be ready?" Georgia asked.

"I guess around six thirty. My call shouldn't last more than an hour. Is Nikki coming by?"

Nikki Peyton was our next-door neighbor. Of course, living where we did, our next-door neighbor was actually a half mile away, but Nikki and her older brother, Tanner, were about the best neighbors I had ever had.

"She hasn't called to say she won't be here, so I am assuming she will. I told her to just stop by when she got off work. If you are still working when she gets here, she can go with me to walk Ramos while the casserole is baking."

"Sounds good. Holler if you need anything."

I closed myself into my bedroom, which also served as my office, turned on my computer, and pulled up the file in which I had been keeping outlines, timetables, character names, and series ideas. I knew that as my agent, Kate would want to see that I had a business plan to market the book once it was complete, and I wanted to show her that Abby the heartbroken widow had found her peace and Abby the hardworking author was back. I knew that getting back to the point where I was with my career before my husband and infant son were killed in the auto accident would not be an easy task, but I'd found a new purpose and direction in my life after moving to Maine, buying the house on the bluff, and meeting Georgia, Rufus, and Ramos.

I heard voices in the kitchen and assumed that Nikki had arrived. Although Georgia was a good decade older than her, the two had really hit it off, and Nikki was spending as much time here with us as she did at the dog training ranch her brother owned just down the coast. A scratch at the door let me know that Rufus wanted to hang out in here with me, so I opened the door to allow the huge orange cat to enter.

"Smart cat," I said as he began to purr. "You know now that Nikki is here it's going to get giggly out there."

"Meow."

I picked Rufus up, gave him a scratch under the chin, and then set him on the bed. "You can hang with me, but you have to let me work. There will be no jumping up and stretching out on my keyboard while I am trying to write. Got it?"

"Meow."

"Okay, great. I'm glad we understand each other."

I sat down at my computer and took a moment to gather my thoughts. I hadn't published a single thing since the accident, and I knew how important this book was. Part of me was terrified to finish it and turn it over to Kate for scrutiny, but another was excited about revisiting this particular chapter of my life.

I picked up my cell and dialed Kate's number in New York at exactly five.

"Abby," Kate greeted. "I see you are right on time."

"I know how valuable your time is and didn't want to keep you waiting. How is New York?"

"Cold. I assume Maine is much the same."

"Maine is cold all wrapped up with breathtakingly beautiful, which, in my opinion, is the best sort of cold."

Kate laughed. "You can keep your awesome views. I'm sure they are spectacular, but I still wouldn't trade them for my nightlife. How is the novel coming along?"

"Good. Better than good. Great, even. I am more than halfway done and I know exactly where I am going with it. I should have it to you in a month or so, along with a rough outline for the next two books in the series."

Kate paused before answering. "That is such good news, Abby. I can't tell you how happy I am to have you back."

"And I'm happy to be back. Were you able to read the pages I sent you last week?"

"I did and I loved them."

I slowly let out the breath I'd been holding in anticipation of her answer. I couldn't believe how nervous I'd been about sending in new pages for the first time in a very long time.

"I'm going to send them back with a few suggestions, which are really nothing more than ideas to consider as you work."

"Thanks. I'll look over your notes as soon as I get them. I'm hoping to get back on the book release schedule with my old publisher."

"If the book as a whole is as good as the sample pages you sent, we shouldn't have any problem selling the series to them. It's really good, Abby. Well done."

"That's great news. Thank you so much. I can't tell you how much this means to me."

I chatted with Kate for a while longer and then hung up and hugged my arms around my body. "We're back," I whispered to myself. Rufus must have realized it was time to celebrate because he got up off the bed and jumped into my lap.

A year ago I hadn't wanted to go on living and now I couldn't wait to see what the future would hold. It really was amazing, I thought to myself, how much difference a year and a change in scenery could make.

Chapter 3

I guess turning four was a big deal in the Parker household because it looked as if half the residents of Holiday Bay had turned out to celebrate Meghan and Mary's birthday. It was much too cold to hold the event outdoors, and the Parker house was not quite large enough to comfortably accommodate so many guests, so Lonnie and Lacy had decided to rent out the local arcade and pizza joint. It was loud, and crowded, and actually kind of perfect.

"I'm so glad you both could come." Lacy hugged both Georgia and me. "It means the world to us that you can share this day with the girls."

I looked around the room, which had been decorated with balloons and streamers. "Did you rent out the building for the entire day?"

"No, just for three hours. I'm giving everyone tokens to play the games, and the pizzas will be served in a few minutes and will keep coming out until everyone has had their fill." Lacy looked over her shoulder. "If you aren't into video games or four-year-olds, a group of adults have gathered in the bar. I'm fine with that as long as everyone gathers together for the cake and presents."

"I see Nikki in the arcade, so I think I'll join her," Georgia said, setting the gifts she had brought on a table that was already overflowing with presents.

"And I think I'll head back to the bar," I added after setting my own gifts on the table.

Lacy handed Georgia a cup full of tokens, which she happily accepted as I turned and went down the short hallway that housed a bathroom and a small office and separated the main eating area and arcade from the bar. When I arrived, I glanced around, eventually deciding to sit in the empty chair at the table occupied by Chief of Police Colt Wilder, who was casually dressed and so looked to be off duty, Lonnie, and Tanner Peyton.

"Mind if I join you?" I asked the men.

"Have a seat." Lonnie got up and pulled out my chair.

"Is Georgia with you?" Tanner asked.

I nodded at the man I suspected was quite smitten with my bubbly roommate. "She's in the front, playing video games with Nikki and the kids."

"Can I get you a beer?" Lonnie asked.

I nodded. "I could go for a beer." I turned to Colt as Lonnie got up to fetch my beverage. "Are you off duty today?"

Colt nodded. "I have coverage for the weekend. I can't believe that Meghan and Mary are already four. It seems like yesterday I was helping Lonnie deliver them in a snowstorm."

I raised a brow. "You delivered the twins?"

Colt nodded. "Lonnie and I did. It was snowing, and not just a little; we are talking a full-on blizzard. Lacy had gone into labor almost a month early, so Lonnie dropped the triplets off with his mother and headed to the hospital in Portland. He hadn't even made it to the main highway when he slipped on some ice and ended up in a ditch. Their cell service was out, but by the grace of God, I happened to be on my way back into town after responding to an accident on the highway. Lacy was ready to give birth by the time I got there, and poor Lonnie was frantic, especially because the twins were early. I used the radio in my car to call for an ambulance, but by the time it showed up, Lonnie and I had helped Lacy to deliver two perfect baby girls."

"Wow," I said, smiling at Lonnie as he set a mug of beer in front of me. "That's really some story."

"What it was, was terrifying," Lonnie said. "There is so much that can go wrong when twins are born, and delivering premature twins is even riskier. But it all worked out. By the time Mary was born, the ambulance had shown up, and it whisked Lacy and both babies to the hospital. They stayed there a couple of nights for observation, but they were healthy despite their tiny size." Lonnie glanced at Colt. "When Colt pulled up just as Meghan's head was crowning and basically took over, I felt like a man on death row who had been given an eleventh-hour reprieve."

"Were Meghan and Mary the first babies you ever delivered?" I asked Colt.

"No. Before I went into law enforcement, I was a field medic in the Army. You would think that delivering babies would fall outside my job description, but, surprisingly, it did not."

"And I for one am grateful for that," Lonnie offered up his glass in a toast to Colt.

I glanced up as Lacy walked into the bar. "Lonnie honey, can you help me get the kids settled in with slices of the first batch of pizzas? I started with cheese so we could feed the kids first."

"Sure thing." Lonnie stood up. He glanced back at the rest of us still sitting at the table. "Finish your beers. You'll want to eat after the kids have finished."

I took a sip of my beer and glanced at Tanner as he stood up as well.

"I think I'll join Nikki and Georgia until it is time to eat," Tanner said.

"Is there something going on between Tanner and Georgia?" Colt asked after he left the bar.

"Yes and no. It seems obvious to me that Tanner is interested in my perky roommate, but it has only been a year since she lost her husband. I don't think she is ready for a romantic relationship with anyone yet. She does enjoy spending time with both Nikki and Tanner, and I suspect that a romance is in their future, when Georgia is ready. I guess only time will tell if things will work out for them."

"Tanner is a great guy, but I understand Georgia's hesitancy. I heard her husband committed suicide."

I nodded. "Yes. He was convicted of embezzling money from his clients, and rather than facing time in prison, he decided to end his life. Poor Georgia lost everything: her husband, her business, her home, and her savings. It must have been very difficult to deal with such a complete annihilation of her life, and she sort of lost herself for a while, but somehow she found her way back to the lively and energetic blond-haired pixie we know and love today."

"Tanner is a good guy. If she needs time, he will give it to her. How about you? Any romance on your horizon?"

I laughed. "Absolutely not. I am hanging on most of the time and even enjoying life on occasion, but I am not in any way ready to go there." I paused and then continued. "If I am out of line for asking, just say so, but while we are on the subject of personal tragedies, I have to say that I am curious about yours. I remember you saying that at the time Carrie Long went missing, you were so tied up in a personal crisis that you didn't follow up the way you should have."

Colt's face hardened just a bit. "My sister and her husband were killed in a car accident at around the time Carrie went missing."

"Oh, no. I'm so very sorry. That must have been devastating. Did they have children?"

Colt nodded. "A boy and a girl. The kids lived with me immediately after the accident, but I live in a small, one-bedroom apartment, and I just wasn't equipped to raise two young children, so we decided that they would live with my parents. I think that situation is really best for everyone, although I do wonder at times if I'm letting my sister down by not stepping up."

"Your parents want to raise the children?"

"They do. They are retired and live on a nice piece of property north of here. The kids are happy living with them, and I make time to visit when I can."

"It sounds like you all made the best decision."

Colt sighed. "I hope so." He took a sip of his beer. "I have been thinking of finding a house. Three bedrooms at least. Something close to town, with a yard. That way the kids can have their own space when they come to visit."

"Do they visit often?" I asked.

Colt shrugged. "Not really. I go up to my parents to see them as often as I can, but I'd like to have them with me here more often. My parents had definite plans for their retirement before my sister died, many of which have been put on hold, but I'm going to make a point of trying to take vacation time that corresponds with trips they'd like to take. Last October I stayed at their place while they went on a Caribbean cruise. My mom really would like to tour Italy in the spring, so I am going to work it out to stay with the kids for three weeks while they are away. It would be easier to have them here. I could find someone to watch them during the day, and I wouldn't have to take as much time off work."

"I think a house sounds like a wonderful idea."

Colt shared with me some of the homes he had looked at to date. We talked about what he'd liked about each property and what he hadn't. He mentioned that he wanted to take his time and find the perfect place, and I assured him that I agreed with that decision because he would probably need to live with whatever he chose for quite some time. We were just starting on the second round of beers when Colt's phone dinged. I could see that he'd received a text, but I didn't want to be rude enough to attempt to see what it said. His frown deepened as he read what was written.

"Is something wrong?" I asked.

Colt looked around the bar. The second round of pizzas had been announced, and everyone other than Colt and me and a group of four men I didn't know who were sitting at a table across the room had left. "It's a friend of mine who works as a medical examiner in another state. After everything that went on last month, I asked him if he would be willing to take a look at Karen Stinson's autopsy report."

"And...?" I asked. Karen had gone hiking alone the previous July and had apparently slipped and fallen from the top of some falls to a river below. She'd drowned, and while it was ruled an accident, new information had come to light during the murder investigation of another local girl, this past December, that had led some of us, including me, to suspect that Karen's death might not have been an accident at all. I hadn't realized that Colt planned to look into it further, but I was glad that he had.

"Karen's right ulna was broken. When the coroner did the autopsy, she attributed the broken arm to the fall, but my friend thinks the break was the result of a defensive wound that could have occurred if she held her right arm in front of her face or body to ward off a blow."

"So someone might have pushed her or hit her with something such as a log that sent her tumbling to her death."

Colt hadn't looked up from his phone, but he did nod to me. "It looks like that could be a possibility. The official cause of death is drowning. Both the coroner and my friend agree on that. The coroner did find a bump on Karen's head that she attributed to the fall and said may or may not have caused her to black out. My friend agrees that Karen was most likely unconscious when she drowned."

"So are you going to reopen the case?" I wondered.

"I don't have enough to do that based on what I have at this point, but I think I will do some unofficial digging." Colt looked at me. "I'd like to keep this between us right now, at least until I have a chance to follow up with some ideas. If it looks like there is a real possibility that Karen was murdered, I will, of course, formally reopen the case, but I just don't feel I can justify the uproar that will result if it is suspected that Karen was murdered with only what I currently have."

I nodded. "I totally understand. I won't say anything to anyone. But you have piqued my interest, so in exchange for my silence, would it be possible to keep me in the loop as you continue your search?"

Colt hesitated. "I suppose that would be acceptable. Give me a few days and we'll talk about it again."

"Yes, that will be fine, and don't worry, I won't say a word." I glanced toward the main room, where everyone else seemed to have gathered. "Should we brave the crowd and grab some pizza?"

"I would suggest we grab a burger down the street instead, but Lacy would skin me alive if I left early, so yes, I would love some pizza."

After Colt and I each grabbed a couple of pieces, we sat down near Lonnie and Lacy, who were chatting with an older woman I'd met before but whose name I couldn't remember.

"Abby, have you met Willa Baker?" Lacy asked.

"I think we have. At the candy shop during the Christmas Festival," I answered.

"Of course. You are the writer who bought the old mansion on the bluff."

"That's right. My business partner, Georgia Carter, and I spoke to you about our plan to open an inn."

Willa smiled. "I do remember the conversation. You know the place used to be run as a resort?"

"Yes," I answered. "I had heard that. I bet it was really something special."

She nodded. "When I was a little girl, I remember sneaking over the fence late at night and swimming in their pool. Of course, using the pool if you weren't a guest of the resort was forbidden, and I suppose I would have gotten into a whole lot of trouble had I been caught, but the allure of the dark, cool water on a hot summer night was more than I could resist."

I knew the pool had been destroyed in a storm more than sixty years ago, so I supposed Willa must be in her seventies now at the very least, although from her looks, I would have guessed the eighties.

"I don't suppose you plan to install a pool?" Willa asked.

"No," I answered. "A pool is not part of the plan. Although I'm not against the concept. The house needs a lot of work, so that is where I am focusing my time and resources at the moment."

"Totally understandable. I've heard that you plan to have theme weekends once you open."

I nodded. "Yes, theme weekends and holiday events are a couple of the things we've discussed."

"I'm not sure if you know this, but I've heard stories that when Jasper and Joslyn Jones first opened the resort back in the thirties, they held gangster weekends."

I lifted a brow. "Gangster weekends?"

"Folks would choose roles such as gangster, barmaid, sheriff, or whatever, and then dress for the part. Men who chose to be gangsters would wear three-piece suits, fedoras, and trench coats, and the women who accompanied them would wear fancy dresses, feather boas, and long gloves. Of course, the barmaids would dress in skimpy costumes with garters and lacy tights, and those who chose to dress as townsfolk would dress appropriately. Everyone would be given a fictitious name and a back story, which would read a lot like the plot of *Bonnie and Clyde*. It was just a fun way for guests to live out any fantasies they might have. From what I understand, they had a lot of fun, and the weekends pulled in a lot of people from out of the area."

"I like the idea of a gangster weekend where everyone dresses and acts the part. We have considered murder mystery weekends, but other themes from the past really hadn't occurred to me. Thanks for sharing your story."

Willa grinned. "Happy to. Been around longer than most, so I have a whole lot of stories to tell. If you need some ideas or want to know more about the history of the resort, you look me up. We'll have tea and get acquainted."

"I'd like that very much, and I definitely will call."

Chapter 4

Four days after the twins' birthday, I was sitting at the kitchen table working on my computer when Georgia walked in with Ramos. She had a fistful of mail, so I assumed she had walked down to the box at the end of the long drive. Given the distance from the house to the mailbox, I had considered getting a post office box in town, but so far I hadn't gotten around to it, so either Georgia or I made the trek to the road every weekday.

"How was the walk?" I asked as Georgia tossed the pile of mail on the kitchen counter.

"Absolutely divine. The air is crisp, the sky sunny, and the sea calm. It may feel like a winter day, but it looks like summer. Well, with the exception of all the snow on the ground." Georgia took off her jacket and hung it on the rack.

"It looks like we have a lot of mail today," I said, nodding toward the pile on the counter.

Georgia pulled off her knit cap and stuffed it into her jacket pocket. "Mostly ads and bills, but there is one envelope made out to the Inn at Holiday Bay that I am dying to open."

"So let's do it."

Georgia pulled off her heavy boots, then crossed the room in her stocking feet and sat down at the table across from me. She reached out to hand me the envelope.

"You can go ahead and open it," I said. "After all, you are the one who schlepped all the way out to the road to get it."

Georgia grinned, then slit open the envelope with a thumbnail. "It is an inquiry from a woman who wants to have her wedding here in September." Georgia looked up at me. "On one hand, I am thrilled to have a request for such a large booking, but on the other, I am also hesitant."

"Yes," I agreed. "I don't see any way we won't be up and running by September, but we are dealing with a major renovation, and really, once you start tearing out walls and replacing plumbing and electrical, anything can happen."

Georgia bit her lip. "Should I call to tell her we can't?"

I was really torn. "How did she hear about us anyway?"

Georgia looked back down at the sheet of paper in her hand. "It says here that she was in town for the Christmas Festival and mentioned to several people that she wanted to get married in Holiday Bay in the fall. She said everyone she spoke to recommended the inn, so she drove by and was drawn in, not only by the location but by the romantic history of the place."

"Romantic history? I'd be more apt to refer to the history of the inn as somewhat tragic."

Georgia shrugged. "I suppose that tragedy and romance can go together. The man who built the place did in fact do it for his one true love."

"A true love who died four months after he married her," I pointed out.

Georgia looked back down at the paper in her hand. "It's odd that this woman didn't just email her inquiry."

"I guess a true romantic might see the artistry of a handwritten note," I suggested.

"I suppose." Georgia set the paper down on the table. "What should I do?"

"Does she want to book the inn for the beginning or the end of September?"

"The end. The last weekend, in fact. The area will be lovely then. The weather should be good, barring rain, and the leaves should be in full color."

I sat back and considered the situation. "Why don't you call her to explain the situation? Let her know that if we are open, which we very much plan to be, we would love to host her wedding, but remind her of the unpredictability of any sort of construction. If she is willing to agree to what I guess we can refer to as a soft booking, let her know that we are willing to reserve the dates, but we will wait to collect a deposit until we get a bit closer. I would even be willing to provide a contract of sorts as long as there are contingencies for us actually being up and running. If she will book under this set of circumstances, I say we do it; if not, I think we should pass."

Georgia nodded. "Agreed. That sounds like a wonderful plan."

I returned my attention to the computer, and Georgia got up to pour herself a cup of coffee. After starting a fresh pot, she returned to the table. "Are you working on your book?"

"No, something else." I paused and looked up. "Remember when we stopped by Tanner's yesterday to pick Nikki up for our shopping excursion?"

"Yeah. What about it?"

"And Tanner's Aunt Charlee was there and Nikki was chatting with her, so she wasn't quite ready to go?"

"Of course. I went out to the barn to see the new, potential FEMA arrivals, and Nikki went upstairs to change. So?"

"While you were both otherwise occupied, I took advantage of the opportunity to ask Charlee, who has lived in Holiday Bay as long as Velma, about Velma's sister."

Georgia raised a brow. "Velma has a sister? She's never mentioned her to me."

"Well, she did to me. She doesn't talk about her much because they haven't spoken in over thirty years."

Georgia looked confused. "Whyever not?"

I leaned back and settled in, in preparation for what I suspected would turn into a long conversation. "It seems that Velma's sister was in love with the same man as Velma. He chose Velma, so the sister left town. Velma hasn't seen or heard from her since."

"That's awful."

I nodded. "It is. My situation with Annie has made it very clear to me that family is more important than almost anything else, and long-standing feuds should not be allowed to fester and grow until they become unmanageable. I told Velma as much and suggested that she should be the one to contact her sister, but she didn't know where she was or how to find her. The situation has been on my mind since I first heard about it, so when I realized that I was alone in a room with a woman who may have more of the details, I took advantage of it to ask her about it."

Georgia crossed her hands on the table. "And...?"

"Charlee told me that Velma's sister's name was Regina Upton, but everyone called her Reggie. She was just twenty-six when she left town, and Charlee thought it was more like thirty-five years ago when it happened, so she estimates that Reggie would be sixty-one or sixty-two today. Before she left, Reggie was dating a man named Adam Miller, and from what Charlee could remember, it seemed that the couple were quite serious. There was even talk of an engagement in the near future, but then Adam met Velma, who had been away at college and recently graduated."

"Let me guess," Georgia said. "Adam and Velma hit it off, and Adam dumped Reggie and hooked up with her younger sister."

"Basically. When Velma and Adam became engaged, Reggie decided she wasn't going to stay around to watch her sister marry the man she loved, so she took off. Velma told me that she thought Reggie would cool off and, once she had some perspective, she would see that Velma and Adam were meant to be together and come home, but she never did."

Georgia frowned. "That is so sad. Velma isn't married now, so what happened to Adam?"

"Velma told me that they did get married, but that it only lasted a few years. He is long gone from her life, which she seemed happy about. I know this is none of my business, but as I said, my situation with my sister has me looking at relationships a lot more seriously. I decided that it couldn't hurt to see if I could track Reggie down. I don't have a lot to go on: a maiden name that probably isn't the name she is going by anymore and a few other small hints that will most likely go nowhere."

Georgia wrapped her hands around her warm cup. "I assume you are doing a Google search for Regina Upton?"

I nodded. "I am. It's early yet, but so far no luck. I asked Charlee if she knew where Regina might have gone when she left Holiday Bay, and she told me that Velma and Reggie had an aunt who lived in Oregon named Maddie Westmore. Reggie talked about her quite often and might have gone to stay with her. I thought I'd try to see if she still is alive and living out west. It isn't a lot to go on, but it is something."

"Have you found out anything else?"

I nodded. "Charlee said that Reggie was the shy, introverted, awkward sister, while Velma was the gregarious, animated one who everyone noticed. It seems Adam wasn't the first man who Velma had taken away from Reggie, and had Reggie not left town, he might not have been the last."

"So there was a history of conflict between the two, even before Adam."

I nodded. "It sounds that way. I spoke to Gilda from Gilda's Café, who has been around for quite a while, but not as far back as when Reggie lived here and had never met her. Though she did say that she had heard that the one subject on which Reggie completely outshone Velma was intellectually. She'd heard that Reggie had gone to work at some big university; it might have been Harvard or Princeton, but she wasn't certain. It's not a lot, but I suppose that gives me another place to look for her."

"Does Velma know you are looking for her sister?" Georgia asked.

"No," I admitted.

"Do you think you should discuss it with her before you go any further?"

"I thought about telling her what I was doing, but I was afraid she would tell me not to get involved. And maybe I shouldn't. But Velma's story really hit home with me and I wanted to do something to help reunite the sisters if I was able. I know that Velma's relationship with her sister is probably none of my business, and she might not be happy that I am getting involved, but when she told me about Regina, I could see the regret and the longing in her eyes. I understand those emotions."

Georgia's expression softened. "I know this is hitting close to home for you. How are things going with Annie? Have you heard from her at all?"

"Not since Ben's birthday."

Georgia raised a brow. "Ben had a birthday recently? Why didn't you say anything?"

"It was a couple of weeks ago, and I didn't say anything because I was trying not to get mired in the depression that had set up camp in a corner of my mind."

"I get that. I probably would have done the same thing. So you heard from Annie then?"

I nodded. "She sent me a one-sentence email that just said that she was thinking of me. I replied to the email that same day and made it very clear that I was touched that she had reached out. I told her I was sorry for everything that had come between us and hoped that we could one day be friends again. I said that I loved and missed her and that my life felt incomplete without her in it. I hoped that she'd email right back, maybe even call, but she didn't. I've sent her two emails since then, even called and left a chatty voicemail, but she hasn't replied."

"I'm sorry that she didn't get back to you." Georgia hugged me. "I know this has been very hard. Still, the fact that she reached out on a day she knew would be difficult for you shows that she still cares. If she didn't care, she wouldn't have gotten in touch at all."

I shrugged. "Yeah. I guess. I just wish this didn't have to be so difficult. I feel like I am doing what I can to patch things up, but I have no way of knowing whether what I'm doing means anything to her."

Georgia reached out and took my hand in hers. "It will. It may take some time, but eventually it will. I've never met Annie and I can't claim to fully understand the dynamic between you, but my guess is that her heart is longing for you as much as yours is longing for her."

******

Later that afternoon, I was working on my novel when Georgia came in from outside. She had a stack of envelopes in her hand that had been tied together with a piece of twine. "More mail?"

Georgia laughed. "No. The plumber found these in the wall of the library when he opened it up to replace the water line. I haven't opened any of the envelopes, but they look like letters. Old letters."

I reached out and took them. "I wonder how long they have been in the wall."

"Lonnie thought they must have slipped down between the shelves and the wall, so I would say they probably belonged to the last owner, or at least the last one who actually lived in the house."

"The last owners to occupy the house were Jasper and Joslyn Jones," I informed Georgia. "They bought the house in 1932 and ran it as a resort until 1954, when a storm damaged the pool, which had been purported to have healing powers. There have been several owners since, but none lived there."

"I suppose the letters could even have been left there by one of the guests who stayed at the resort," Georgia said. She narrowed her gaze. "The postmarks are all from 1948. Should we open them?"

I nodded. "I don't see why not. It's not as if whoever wrote them is still around to care one way or another." I opened the first envelope and pulled out a single sheet of paper. "It appears that this letter was written by someone named Victor to someone named Ursula."

"Love letters?" Georgia asked.

I passed the paper to Georgia so she could read it herself. While I wouldn't call the letters racy, they were fairly intimate, and I would have felt odd reading such private thoughts out loud. How strange that someone—presumably Ursula—had left a batch of letters on the shelf in the library in the resort in the first place.

"It sounds like Victor and Ursula were having themselves quite the affair." Georgia giggled. "Not that these letters are inappropriate; they are pretty flowery, though." She turned the paper over to read the writing on the back. "The prose style makes this sound as if it was written a lot earlier than 1948. In fact, if we found out that this was written by Chamberlain Westminster, the man who built the house in the late 1890s, it wouldn't surprise me a bit. Don't you think this has a bit of an English flair to it?"

"I suppose that just because the envelopes were postmarked in 1948, that doesn't mean the letters inside them were written then."

Georgia looked at that envelope again. "This one is addressed to Bluff House Spa and Resort. There's a room number, six, but no name to whom it was to be delivered." She looked up. "That seems odd to me. Shouldn't the letter be for Mrs. Jones, or whatever the recipient's name was, care of the Bluff House Spa and Resort, followed by the room number, and then at least the town and the state?"

"You would think so. I suppose that simply adding the room number might have seemed like enough of an address to a local postman seventy years ago. Maybe the recipient was a long-term resident at the resort."

Georgia frowned. "I suppose. Do you mind if I hang on to these? I'd like to read all of them."

"Knock yourself out."

A dreamy look came over Georgia's face. "I suppose the spa would have been a very romantic place to have a fling back in the day. When the guests were pampered. The house must have been divine."

"From what I understand, the place was a real showpiece in its day. Still, an illicit love affair in the resort doesn't interest me the way the romance between Chamberlain Westminster and Abagail Chesterton does, especially with her dying young and leaving him brokenhearted."

Georgia grinned. "I suppose you are right." She looked down at the letter in her hand. "I've always believed that the heart wants what it wants."

Chapter 5

Life can be frustrating. Not just frustrating—infuriating.

While I had been on a roll with my novel and actually thought that I might finish it ahead of schedule, I now found myself totally blocked at the 90 percent point. I was a professional and knew to deal with these temporary blocks, but it had been three days and I had rewritten the same page eight times, which had me believing that this time I wasn't going to be able to find a way out of the corner I'd written myself into. To be honest, at this point I was considering chucking the whole manuscript *and* my laptop into the ocean. In my mind, a burial at sea was the only option left, because I had tried everything else, up to and including pounding my fists energetically on my desk, cursing loudly at the imaginary being who had robbed me of my creativity, and stomping around the room with my arms in the air demanding to know why the universe hated me.

Now I was comparing myself to every other writer on the planet and close to deciding that every single one of them was, in every way, better than I.

I guess you could say that being blocked did not bring out my best qualities.

I had just unplugged the laptop in preparation for its journey to the sea when my phone rang. I looked at the caller ID to see who it was and answered.

"Are you busy?" Colt asked.

"Not even a tiny little bit. What's up?"

"I've been looking in to the details surrounding Karen Stinson's death and I've found enough irregularities to cause me to investigate further. I thought I'd hike up to the falls where she died to take another look. Do you want to come?"

"Hike?" I looked out the window at the three feet of snow on the ground. "You do know that there is snow on the ground, right?"

Colt chuckled. "Yes, I had noticed. I plan to wear snowshoes."

"Snowshoes?"

"Yes. Shoes you secure to your feet that help you walk in the snow. Have you ever tried them?"

"Never." Nor was I the least bit sure I ever wanted to.

"I have an extra pair you can borrow."

I hesitated.

"It's easy. I can show you what to do, and I will even take you to dinner when we get back."

I glanced at my traitor computer and knew that it was unlikely to cooperate with me even if I spent the entire day glaring at it. "Okay," I eventually said. "But keep in mind that I am probably going to suck at walking through the snow on big ping-pong paddles."

"I'll keep that in mind. I have some work to do this morning. How about I pick you up at one?"

"Okay. I'll be ready."

"And dress warmly, but not too warm. Wear layers. I know it seems like you will be cold, but once you start walking, I guarantee you will warm up real fast."

What had I gotten myself in to? "Got it. Lots of layers. I'll see you at one."

Deciding that tossing my laptop into the Atlantic Ocean was no longer going to give me the satisfaction it would have a few minutes before, I headed out into the living area of the cottage, where I found Georgia sitting at the dining table scowling at the stack of letters she had been reading and rereading for days. "I see the mystery of Victor and Ursula is still causing you angst."

Georgia let out a long breath. "Yeah."

"Anything I can help with?" I opened the cupboard, pulled out a mug, and poured myself a fresh cup of coffee.

"In the letters, Ursula refers to a gift that Victor has left with her. At first I figured it was a piece of jewelry or some other item of great value because she seemed to be so focused on it, but after reading the letters about a million times, I'm beginning to think the gift must be something else."

"Something else like a car, or maybe a fur coat?"

"Something else like a baby."

I frowned and sat down. "A baby? Are you sure?"

"Actually, no. The letters that were found are mostly from Victor to Ursula, but there are several that look to be from Ursula to Victor. I am assuming that it was Ursula who left the letters in the library, so

I don't know why she would have had letters she had written and sent to Victor unless she tried to mail them to him, but they were undeliverable."

"You think he knocked her up and then left her here at the resort to have the baby on her own?"

Georgia shrugged. "Maybe. I can't tell for sure. The letters written from Ursula to Victor do make it sound as if she either doesn't know where he is or she can't reach him for some reason."

I took a sip of my coffee. "Okay, so what makes you think the gift that Victor left Ursula was a baby?"

Georgia picked up one of the letters and looked at it. "Ursula seems to care a great deal about the gift Victor left her. I get the feeling that it has become the most important thing in her life. She seems to genuinely feel love for it, but I also get the sense that she is afraid for it. I suppose if Victor left her some big ol' diamond, she might feel the same way, but I think her feeling for the gift goes deeper than that. Unless Ursula was a very shallow person, a baby is the only thing I could come up with."

I sat back and considered this. I supposed that a woman in the 1940s could have become pregnant out of wedlock just as easily as a woman today. "Are you certain that Victor and Ursula weren't married?"

"I don't think so, although it doesn't say anything about it anywhere in the letters. After reading through them dozens of times, it appears to me that Victor might be married to someone named Harriet." Georgia sorted through the pile of letters, eventually settling on one. "This letter is from Victor to Ursula. It says: 'Harriet must never learn of the gift. It would destroy her. I know the sacrifice is considerable, but it is a sacrifice we must be willing to make.'"

"So, it appears as if Victor, a married man, had an affair with Ursula, whose marital status is unknown," I began to summarize, "and that affair resulted in a gift, which you believe to be a baby. Ursula seemed to be staying at the house back when it was a spa, and by the end of the letter trail, it seemed as if she no longer was able to reach Victor, leading to the assumption that he dumped her and took off."

Georgia nodded. "While the letters are cryptic, with everything implied but never actually stated, from what I have been able to decipher thus far, that would be my best guess."

"I wonder what happened to the baby."

Georgia frowned. "I don't know. But I am motivated enough to try to find out."

"I saw Willa Baker at the Parker twins' birthday party, and she told me how she used to climb the fence and swim in the spa pool when she was a kid. I wonder if she would remember a pregnant woman staying here. It sounds like Ursula must have been here for a while, so it's possible Willa might have seen her."

Georgia's eyes grew large. "Will you ask her to talk to me about her?"

"I don't have Willa's phone number, but I'll call Lacy to see if she can set up a meeting with Willa for tomorrow, or as soon as possible after that. Right now, I am getting ready to go snowshoeing."

"Snowshoeing?"

"With Colt. I've never tried it, but according to him, it's easy."

Georgia laughed. "I tried it once and it was not easy, but maybe you will do better at it than I did. My legs are so dang short that I kept tripping myself up."

I glanced down at my own legs. They were longer than Georgia's, but I wasn't really any more coordinated than her. I hoped I wasn't going to regret agreeing to Colt's little outing.

I glanced at the clock and realized I had over an hour before I needed to start getting ready for it, though, so I decided to check in with Lonnie. The remodel was moving along so quickly that I was afraid I'd miss an important stage in the transformation if I didn't pop over every day or two.

"Just the woman I wanted to see," Lonnie greeted me as I walked into my brand-new kitchen through the back door.

"What's up?"

"First of all, I spoke to Bobby, and he has us scheduled in two weeks for the refurbishment of the mantel and the creation of the new crown molding for the dining area, which, he assures me, you will not be able to tell apart from the original crown molding that is undamaged and has been here since it was installed when the house was built in the eighteen hundreds."

I smiled. "That's wonderful. The first thing I saw when I walked into the house on the day I first arrived was that mantel. I knew it would need to be preserved."

"Bobby will bring her back to life. Which brings me to the mantel in the library. It is not as intricate as the one in the living room but still very old, and I thought we could strip and stain it rather than paint over it as we initially discussed."

"Will Bobby have time to tackle it as well?"

"Probably not, but the design is much simpler. I was thinking of asking Lacy if she wanted to take a stab at restoring it. If you are open to the idea and she is willing, I figured she could find a sitter for Maddie while the older five are in school in the mornings."

"I've seen Lacy's work and it is perfection. If she is interested in tackling the job, go for it."

Lonnie nodded. "I'll talk to her about it this evening, but I think she will be thrilled to have the opportunity. If we decide to sand and stain and not paint, you will need to choose a stain. Actually, now that we are going to replace the shelving in the library, you are going to need to look at a stain anyway. It would look nice if the shelving and mantel matched."

"I agree. Send me some swatches along with a few suggestions and I'll take a look. How is the downstairs bath coming?"

Lonnie grinned. "It's done." He took my hand. "Come on and I'll show you."

I followed him into the suite that was originally going to be the manager's suite but Georgia and I had decided to rent out for the time being at least. I'd chosen varying shades of blue for the room, which had worked out to be simply amazing.

"Wow. Look at that shower."

The shower was lined in a deep, royal blue granite, while the shower pan, as well as the floor in the large room, had been tiled with wood grain planks. The walls were painted light blue and the whole room was framed with white molding along the ceiling and floor.

"Four heads, just like we discussed," Lonnie said. "It will feel like showering under a waterfall."

The Jacuzzi tub was tucked into a nook, with a window looking out to the sea. It was white, but I could imagine how it would look once I'd stacked deep blue towels along the rim. The cabinets where the double sinks were located were topped with the same blue granite as the shower, and the commode was tucked into its own small room so that it could be used at the same time someone else was taking a soak in the tub.

"The bedroom walls are painted, the wood floors laid, and the fireplace tiled with white," Lonnie added.

"I know I'd want to stay in this room," I said. I walked into what would be the seating area of the suite. "In fact, I'm pretty sure Georgia is going to change her mind about living in the guest room in the cottage once she sees this."

"Georgia has seen the room, and while I do think she is a little bit in love with what we have created, she is totally committed to making a go of the inn and realizes that having six rooms to rent out will make all the difference."

"Georgia is really great," I said. "How are the rooms on the second floor coming along?"

"We're moving right along. The two suites on the second floor will be laid out much like this one. The plumbing and electrical are being seen to next week. Once that is all in, we can begin with the floors, walls, and closets. Have you decided on colors for the two second-floor suites? I know you said you wanted them all to be different."

"I think I'd like the suite on the right to have medium gray cabinets because I found that dark green granite for the shower and countertops in the bathroom. The granite has gray running through it, so I think it will tie together nicely."

"The granite really is striking. Some of the most unique I have ever seen."

I took a few steps away from Lonnie and looked out the huge picture window, which would bring the sea in to both the sleeping and sitting area. "I'm thinking wood grain tile planks for the bathroom, maybe in light gray, and hardwood floors for the sleeping and sitting area. Maybe we should just use the same hardwood flooring through the entire house."

"I agree with that as well," Lonnie said. "You discussed a room done in black and white. Do you want that suite on the second floor or the third?"

"I think I will save the black and white for the attic, although I may very well change my mind by the time we get to that point. We are adding a lot of windows up there, so there will be plenty of color coming in from the outside if we do decide to go with that option."

"Sounds good. Have you decided on colors for suite two on the second floor?"

"We are using dark green and light gray for suite one, so maybe we can use sage green and a dark gray for suite two. The areas will have their own feel, but I think that a similar color pallet would provide consistency. I still haven't worked out the colors for the third floor, but I suppose we have time before we need them."

Lonnie nodded. "We are removing and replacing a lot of walls on the second floor, so it will take a while. Especially with the plumbing upgrades and fireplace additions we have planned. Still, it doesn't hurt to keep tossing around ideas so that you are ready when we need them."

"I'll chat with Georgia about it. She has a lot of good ideas." I glanced at my watch. "I need to run. I'm going snowshoeing with Colt."

Lonnie chuckled. "Be sure to wear layers you can peel off. It will start off cold, but I promise you, by the time you have been walking for fifteen minutes you will begin to get hot."

Chapter 6

"You're kidding, right?" I stood with my mouth open, staring at the huge snowshoes Colt held. "Don't you have shorter ones? There is no way I can walk in those."

"When we begin to climb, the snow is going to get deep. You'll need the larger pair. You'll be fine once you get used to them."

I didn't think so, but Colt was a cop, so I doubted he was trying to kill me. I sat down on a large rock from which he had cleared the snow while he strapped the monstrosities onto my boots. I had a feeling that I would be walking with a limp tomorrow, if I was able to walk at all. Once my snowshoes were strapped on, Colt strapped on his own and then took my hands and pulled me to my feet.

"The secret is to lift your feet into the air when you step. Don't drag them. If you do, you will likely trip. Just lift your leg, take a step forward, and then lower your foot to the ground."

I did as Colt instructed without falling, which was, I guess, something. Of course, he still held both my hands. He told me to repeat what I had done with the other foot and I did.

"See?" he said. "You're doing just fine. Keep going."

"How far are the falls?" I asked.

"A couple of miles to the trailhead that climbs up the backside, and then maybe another half mile."

"So in all, we are going to walk five miles to the falls and back?"

Colt nodded. "Yeah. About that."

I took another step and then paused. "You do realize that even if I manage to make it to the falls and back without breaking my neck, at this pace it is going to take a month."

Colt chuckled. "You will be able to walk at a normal speed when you get used to the shoes. Just keep going, and before you know it, you won't even notice the snowshoes on your feet."

I highly doubted that, but I took another step and then another. Colt let go of one hand and then the other, which terrified me at first, but after I'd taken a dozen or so steps on my own, I began to feel more confident. I was actually doing fairly well as long as I focused on my feet, but then Colt began to explain what he had learned about Karen's death since our last chat and I got distracted and dragged rather than lifted and fell flat on my face.

"Are you okay?" Colt lifted me out of the snow and into his arms.

I spit out the snow that somehow had ended up in my mouth. "Peachy. I guess I just lost focus."

"That's okay, you're doing great. It won't be long before you don't have to think about stepping, not dragging. It will come naturally."

Again, I doubted it. If you asked me, this felt like one of those walking-while-chewing-gum scenarios. I was fine as long as all I did was walk, but introduce a second element and I was toast. I was glad that Colt had suggested layers because once we started to walk, I got very warm, and the layers began to come off. I didn't want to carry them, so I just tossed them onto the snow behind me, figuring I could gather them up on the way back.

By the time we arrived at the trailhead, where we were going to begin to climb, I actually felt like I had the hang of things. I hadn't said a single word since I'd fallen, but I felt I'd found a rhythm and could probably handle both walking and talking, so I asked Colt to fill me in on what he had discovered since we'd last spoken.

"After I found out that the break to Karen's arm could very well have been a defensive wound to ward off her attacker, I went back to the beginning and reinterviewed everyone I had spoken to the first time around. I realized, even as I launched my campaign to talk to the people who knew Karen best, that my effort could very well be fruitless, but when her body had initially been found I had been speaking to folks with the idea that the fall had been nothing more than a terrible accident, so I wasn't looking for motive so much as a timeline."

"And...?" I asked as I stopped after coming to a fallen log. There was no way I was stepping over that without serious injury.

"And at first I found that most folks answered the questions I asked in much the same way that they had the first time." Colt stepped over the log, turned, and offered me a hand. I accepted his hand, lifted my leg as high as I could, and took a huge step over the log. If Colt hadn't been hanging on to me, I was certain I would have experienced my second face-plant of the day, but I was able to land safely on the other side.

"I'm sensing that at some point the answers changed," I said after we started walking again.

"They did. One of Karen's very best friends, a woman named Lily May, mentioned during our second interview that Karen had recently gone through some stuff that had left her feeling pretty devastated. I asked what sort of things had caused her to feel that way, and Lily didn't know, just that the reason Karen went hiking alone was to work through something."

I paused and took several deep breaths. The hike had definitely gotten harder. "Whatever was going on with Karen must have been serious if she didn't confide in her best friend."

"Yes. I think Lily was hurt that Karen seemed to have kept a secret from her. All she would tell Lily was that she needed time to think about things, and try to figure out what she was going to do."

I paused and leaned against a tree. I guessed that I was in worse shape than I thought. "Do about what?"

Colt shrugged. "Again, Lily didn't know. Karen had been upset about something maybe four months before the accident, but she seemed to have been able to work through it. Lily said she appeared to be back to her old self after a period of what seemed like mourning to her, but then Karen started acting even more strangely a few weeks before her fall."

"What does that mean? Even more strangely?"

"Karen seemed to withdraw into herself. She was losing weight and looked like she hadn't been sleeping. Lily asked Karen about it repeatedly, but the only thing that she was willing to share was that a family member had passed away the previous winter and there had been a trickle-down effect that she hadn't been expecting."

"Do you know who died?" I asked.

"Lily didn't, but I plan to do some checking. Karen's father died when she was young and her mother died a couple of years ago. As far as I know, she was an only child, but I didn't dig into her family history all that much when she fell. I know that a cousin was determined to be her next of kin, so I am assuming that there weren't any siblings or grandparents in the picture then." Colt paused, adjusted the strap on his snowshoe, and then continued. The terrain was getting even steeper, so maintaining a conversation was going to be tough. At least for me. Colt seemed to be unaffected by the effort required to make the climb. "Anyway, Lily didn't know what was wrong with Karen, so I kept digging around and found out from another friend, Gloria Dover, that Karen had told her that she was thinking about moving. Gloria thought that Karen was happy in Holiday Bay and asked her why. Karen said that she needed a change of scenery."

"Sounds like guy trouble to me."

"That was my first thought as well." Colt stopped walking so that I could catch up. "Just another quarter mile."

A quarter mile wasn't all that far unless you were walking straight uphill. I looked behind me and wondered how in the heck I was going to get back down this hill without rolling end over end. Maybe Colt *was* trying to kill me.

"So, did you find out if Karen had a guy in her life?" I asked, trying desperately to focus on something other than the fact that my legs felt like jelly and I was sure they were about to crumple beneath me.

"I asked around, but none of Karen's friends knew of a man, so I decided that her emotional state must have been based on something other than a love affair gone bad." Colt stopped walking, pulled some low-lying branches aside, and gestured for me to move on. "I still don't know what that something might have been, but I have a few more friends to talk to," he added after he continued on behind me.

"Okay, so Karen seemed to be going through something in the weeks before she fell to her death, but we don't know what. Anything else?" I paused and gasped for air. Holy Moses, my lungs were burning. Of course, the burning in my lungs didn't compare to the burning in my legs, which, as it turned out, was even worse than the jelly feeling. I seriously had no idea how I was going to go on. If we didn't reach the top soon, Colt was going to have to go the rest of the way on his own.

"I'm afraid my interviews didn't net me a lot of information that I didn't already have," Colt went on. "I checked Karen's financials and there wasn't any unusual activity in the weeks leading up to her fall, and I took another look at her phone records, which seemed normal as well. There was one charge on her credit card for a plane ticket, but I later learned that she had bought the ticket for a friend who was broke and needed to fly home to see her mother, who was in the final stages of cancer."

"Aw, that was nice."

"So what do you think?" Colt asked.

Think? I was breathing so hard, I couldn't even ask what he meant, but then I looked ahead and what breath that remained in my lungs, which wasn't a lot, escaped. "Wow." We'd made it to the top of the falls. There was a layer of ice on the outermost surface of the falls, which made it appear as if the whole thing was frozen clear through, but I could hear water running beneath the ice, which created a beautiful yet sort of eerie sound.

"Isn't it something? The water on the exterior of the falls freezes, but the water beneath the ice continues to flow." Colt pointed to the river below. "It too appears frozen, but only on the surface. If you punch through the ice, you find the water. If you follow the stream down a bit, you will come across a beautiful little lake with fantastic ice fishing."

Ice fishing? Regular fishing was bad enough, in my opinion, but who in their right mind would want to sit on the ice trying to catch a fish?

"It's beautiful," I managed, now that we had stopped hiking and my heart rate was beginning to slow.

"It's one of the most beautiful spots in the area in my opinion. I come up here every winter, even when I'm not investigating a case."

"It is really lovely. Thank you for bringing me." I looked over the edge of the falls, hoping that my feet were planted solidly enough that I wouldn't be the next casualty of the steep drop-off. "It's a ways down. Seems like it would be hard to survive the fall."

"There are rocks beneath the water, so surviving isn't likely," Colt agreed.

"If Karen was pushed, what do you think happened? Did someone sneak up behind her or did she hike up here with someone who turned on her?"

Colt's lips tightened. "I don't know, but I intend to find out."

He looked around the area, then took off his snowshoes and walked to the edge of the steep drop. Too close, as far as I was concerned. I wanted to yell for him to be careful, but I didn't want to startle him, so I just held my breath until he took a step back toward me. It wasn't that I was afraid of heights exactly; it was more that I was afraid of falling.

Colt took out his phone and began snapping photos, focusing mainly on the ground. He paused and took a look at what he had taken, then took a few more.

"Are you looking for anything specific?" I asked.

Colt pointed to the trail as it led to the edge of the falls. "The trail levels off after the climb and is flat as you approach the falls and then climbs just a bit at the edge. The incline forms sort of a lip. It seems to me that unless someone stood right on the edge, which isn't likely when the water is flowing, they wouldn't fall into the water below but backward had they stumbled."

I looked at the trail and nodded. "That seems right. Or if you did fall forward, you wouldn't fall far. Do you think this means Karen was pushed?"

Colt turned and looked toward the edge of the falls, although this time he looked only with his eyes and didn't move forward, for which I was grateful. "Now that I am really looking at things, I think it is likely that she was pushed. Unless, of course, she jumped."

"Jumped? You think she committed suicide?"

Colt shrugged. "I really don't know. I didn't know her well enough to make a statement about the state of her mental health at the time she died. Suicide would, however, make more sense than a slip and fall, and her friends did say she had been living in a state of distress."

"What about the broken arm?"

Colt walked back to me. "The defensive wound to the arm does make it appear as if she was attacked. I've been up here a bunch of times but never really noticed the incline at the end of the trail. It makes a natural wall of sorts, which, I would be willing to bet, is why there haven't been more slip and falls here."

He sat down on a rock and began pulling on his snowshoes. "It took longer than I estimated to get up here. We should head back."

"Already?" I'd hoped to rest a bit longer.

"We'll want to get back before it gets dark and we will need to stop along the way to pick up your wardrobe."

I let out a soft groan.

"Don't worry, the trip back will go a lot quicker than the one up."

I had no doubt of that, especially because I'd probably end up sliding down the hill on my backside at least part of the way given the steepness of the terrain.

Chapter 7

When I woke the following morning, I couldn't move. I mean, literally couldn't move. Colt hadn't mentioned that paralysis was going to be a side effect of hiking five miles on snowshoes the very first time I'd tried the dang-blasted things.

Georgia knocked on my door. "Are you okay?"

"I'm fine," I called back.

"It sounds like you're dying or something."

"I am dying." I tried to sit up but ended up flopping back into the pillows. "I definitely think I'm dying. Come on in."

Georgia poked her head around the door. "Can I help?"

"I think I may be paralyzed. Maybe you should call 9-1-1."

Georgia chuckled. "I guess you are feeling the effects of your outing yesterday."

"Effects? Are you trying to tell me this is normal?"

Georgia made her way over to the bed and held out her hands. "Your legs will feel better once you start moving around a bit."

"I don't disagree, but I really can't move."

"Take my hands. I'll pull you up."

I did as Georgia suggested. She pulled on my arms until I was sitting up and then turned me so my legs dangled over the side of the bed. She slid my slippers onto my feet and pulled me into a standing position. She handed me my robe, which I slipped over my pajamas, then offered her arm in support.

"Just take small steps," she said.

"I can't."

"I made French toast."

French toast did sound good and I was hungry. I put my arm around Georgia's shoulder and took a step. Did it hurt? Heck yeah. But then I took another step and another, and before I knew it, I'd made it to the living room, where she had a warm fire, hot coffee, and delicious French toast waiting.

"After you eat you should take a long soak in a hot tub and then you should walk around a bit. Once you loosen up those muscles, you will start to feel better."

I knew Georgia was right. Ben and I had run a marathon when we were in college and I could remember similar pain the following morning.

"Lacy called this morning," Georgia said.

"She did?" I spooned fresh berries onto my French toast. "What did she want?"

"She said that an antique store that she absolutely adores is going out of business so they are having a huge sale. She wondered if we would want to go with her to have a look. I told her I wasn't sure what your schedule was like for today, but that I'd ask you about it and call her back."

I glanced at my bedroom door. I had been planning on a full day of wallowing in self-doubt and yelling at my laptop, but it was possible a break from my manuscript could give me the new perspective I needed. Of course I was going to need a wheelchair to get around, but I was sure that could be arranged. "We do need to start thinking about furniture for the inn. I figure if we find stuff, we can store it in the basement until the remodel is done."

Georgia poured me a second cup of coffee. "So, should I tell her we'll join her?"

"Sure. Why not? You may have to carry me out to the car, though."

Georgia tilted her head just a bit. "I'll run that hot bath for you. I promise, once you get everything warmed up, you'll be good as new."

******

I wouldn't say I was as good as new exactly, but I did feel better, and I even managed to get myself dressed. I did some stretching exercises while Georgia took Ramos out for a quick walk, and by the time Lacy showed up, I actually felt halfway human.

"What a cute jacket," Georgia said to her after giving her a hello hug.

"I got it on clearance when I was in Portland a few weeks ago." Lacy ran her hands up and down the arms of the worn denim garment. "I'd been wanting something cute but casual that didn't scream *mother of six*, and when I saw this, I knew it had to come home with me."

"Well, it is adorable, and it screams *college coed* rather than *mother of six*."

Lacy smiled. "Thanks. That is exactly what I was going for." She glanced at me. "Are you ready?"

"As I'll ever be." I limped toward the car.

Lacy held the back door open for me. "Lonnie told me about your outing with Colt. I can't believe he dragged you all the way up to the falls your first time on snowshoes. I think I may need to have a chat with him. He can be so clueless sometimes."

I slipped into the car and buckled my seat belt. "That's okay. I am feeling the effects of our climb today, but it was really beautiful. I'm glad I went. I had no idea that falls could freeze."

"It is pretty spectacular," Lacy said. "Lonnie and I used to snowshoe up there before we had the kids. Now when we get a free day, we are more about relaxing. Or shopping."

"Is Lonnie watching the kids today?" I asked.

Lacy nodded. "He is settled in with basketball and some snacks, so the three of us have the entire day to shop till we drop."

"Shopping till I drop shouldn't take me more than five minutes." I chuckled.

It was nice spending the day with friends. When I'd lived in San Francisco, Ben and I had a couple of friends, but I can't say I had girlfriends who were just mine. He and I started dating during our third year of college, and looking back, it seemed as if being a couple pretty much defined our lives from that point forward. Not that building a life as a couple hadn't been important to me at the time, but looking back, I realize I'd forgotten how fun having girlfriends could be.

"The antique barn we are going to be visiting has their antiques mixed in with the rest of their secondhand wares," Lacy informed us. "The first time I went there, I was certain I wasn't going to find anything of real value, but I was with a friend who was looking for something specific, so I took a look around, and once I really started to concentrate, I started finding real gems among the trash."

"I don't mind digging through a bunch of junk to find a gem," Georgia said. "I know it can be aggravating, but when you do finally find that jewel, it seems all that much sweeter."

Lacy turned her head slightly. "I know what you mean. You know that federal drop-front tambour desk I have in my entry? I found it wedged between an old desk I was sure originally came from a big-box store and an old oak table that definitely had been mass-produced. Even in the condition the desk was in when I purchased it, it would have gone for over two thousand dollars in an upper-end antique store, but I wound up getting it for four hundred dollars."

I raised a brow. "Seems like quite a find."

"It was." Lacy agreed. "I had to kiss a lot of frogs to find my prince, but it was worth it."

Lacy pulled off the highway onto a narrow country lane. The road had been plowed, but from its width, if another car approached from the opposite direction, someone would have to pull over while the other car passed. After a couple of miles the road widened and a large red barn appeared. The parking area was more of a pasture than a lot, but I found the whole thing charming.

"Wow, I love it," Georgia said. "It's too bad it is closing."

"The owner decided to sell the land and move to Florida. I guess he is tired of the cold. There are times I can understand that sentiment, but most of the time I wouldn't live anywhere but here. Like I said, I have always found treasures here, so don't get discouraged if you encounter what looks to be someone's messy garage when you first walk in. The wooden chair behind that stack of plastic ones could be a big-lot special, or it could be a hundred-year-old antique."

"Speaking of chairs, I still need some for the table you refinished for me."

"We will have a hard time finding enough that match, but I'm thinking that maybe sixteen high-back chairs that don't necessarily match but all are old enough to be considered antiques would look great," Lacy replied. "I'll keep my eye out." She looked at Georgia. "How about you? Is there anything special you are looking for?"

Georgia shook her head. "No. I have everything I need. I just figured it would be fun to come along for the ride."

I knew that Georgia had been pinching pennies since she'd been living with me. I guess I understood that. Life had certainly proved itself to be unpredictable, and I could understand the desire to stash a few dollars away for a rainy day.

The first thing I noticed when I walked through the door of the old barn was that it was crammed so full and things were stacked in such a random fashion that there didn't seem to be any clear path to make your way from one end of the building to the other. Leaning on the wall near the front door was a rusty old bike that I was sure was pretty much worthless, but against the bike was an old toboggan that was quite charming. I'd never been around snow much as a child, but I had seen movies where all the kids from a neighborhood would pile onto one of the wooden propulsion devices before flying down a snowy hill, and I had to admit that it looked like fun, if not somewhat terrifying.

"Oh look, chairs," Lacy said, taking my hand and pulling me forward.

I tried my best to keep up with the tiny imp, but because every step was a challenge, I found myself lagging behind.

"These four here are just old," Lacy walked right past the first grouping we came to, "but these," she ran her hand over one of four matching chairs with peeling stain and a whole lot of scratches. "These are magnificent." Lacy bent down and looked beneath the seat of the chair. "I would say they were built in the early twentieth century. There is some warping, which seems to indicate that they were stored in a damp location. But I think I can fix that." Lacy ran her hand down one leg and up the other. "The craftsmanship is exquisite. I would be willing to bet these chairs were originally commissioned by someone with the money to insist on only the best."

"So you think they would be a good match for the table?" I asked.

Lacy grinned and nodded. "I do. I know we need sixteen chairs, but four is a start, and I think we can find twelve more in a similar style."

"If you are willing to refurbish them, I'm game," I said.

"Great." Lacy looked around. "I'm going to have a chat with Mr. Thompson to settle on a price. I'll see if he will store them, along with whatever else we find. Lonnie can come by with his truck to pick everything up."

"I hate to bother Lonnie with the pickup," I said. "I'm fine to pay for delivery."

"Nonsense. Lonnie won't mind a bit. You go ahead and keep looking and I'll find you once I make a deal for the chairs."

It was clear that Lacy was in her element. I wasn't really the sort to want to barter, but she seemed to think it was part of the game, so I left her to it. I tried to imagine my table with sixteen chairs of a similar style that didn't necessarily match and realized that was going to be just fine.

Georgia had disappeared, so after Lacy walked away I began to meander. I wasn't sure that shopping in a store that was quite this cluttered was my thing, but a bin filled with watercolors, prints, and sketches caught my eye. Some had obviously been mass produced, but others looked to have been hand drawn or painted. There were quite a few watercolors of the marina, several sketches of the landscape in full fall color, and even a small oil painting of the old church that had been built in the late nineteenth century and still stood on a bluff just up the coast. I wasn't really in the market for artwork and was about to walk away when I happened to notice a colorful sketch of the house. My house.

I pulled it out of the pile and then removed it from its frame to take a better look. The sketch was drawn on thick paper that appeared to have aged. The house stood alone on the bluff, so it must have been drawn before the cottage was built. The house was in perfect repair, so I had to assume the drawing had been done soon after it was built.

"Wow, that's the house," Georgia said from behind me. "It's wonderful."

"That's what I was thinking."

Georgia pointed toward a small but legible signature. "'CW, 1896.'"

I frowned. "CW? As in Chamberlain Westminster?"

"Perhaps," Georgia said. "He was, after all, the man who built the house."

"Yes. In 1895. Lonnie told me that his wife, Abagail, died just four months after they were married, and Chamberlain left the United States for England. According to what Lonnie said, he never returned."

"Do you know when Chamberlain and Abagail were married?" Georgia asked. "I mean the month?"

"No."

"I suppose they could have been married in November or December, which would mean that Chamberlain could have done the drawing in January or February of the next year, just before Abagail died."

"I suppose it could have happened that way." I held up the sketch. "Whether CW is Chamberlain Westminster or not, the sketch is perfect. I'm going to have it reframed and then hang it over the fireplace in the living room once the mantel has been refurbished and the room is finished."

Georgia ran a finger down the front of the print. "I wonder if we can find out for certain who drew it. If it was Chamberlain Westminster, and he did it during the four months he lived in the house with the love of his life, that would be kind of wonderful."

"Yes." I nodded. "How romantic it would be if we could prove that the man who drew the house was the same one who built it. I wonder how we can find out."

Georgia looked around. "I doubt the man who owns this place would know, but the sketch is really good, so it stands to reason that CW, whoever he was, must have made other sketches as well. I bet if we take the sketch to a local artist, they might be able to figure out its history. We may even be able to find additional sketches of the house. It would be really special to have sketches scattered around the place."

"I'm going to find Lacy to let her know I want to buy this as well as the chairs. I saw a secretary's desk against the wall I want to take a closer look at too. I don't suppose you noticed any bedroom furniture that may be worthy of a place in our country inn?"

"Not yet, but I'll keep looking. This store does seem to have treasures to find if you are willing to look for them."

Chapter 8

"Wow, it is really coming down out there," Georgia said as she slid a cookie sheet into the oven. "I bet we'll have a couple of feet of new snow before the end of the day."

"I heard we may get up to three feet," I answered. I glanced at the cookies that were cooling on every available countertop. "I thought the bake sale for the children's arts program was over."

"It is," Georgia replied. "I wanted a way to make some extra money while we are waiting for the inn to open, so I talked to Gilda and Velma about providing baked goods for their restaurants. Both were open to the idea, so I agreed to provide a certain number of pies and cakes to each café three times a week."

"That sounds like a great idea, but those look like cookies. Hundreds of cookies."

"While I was at Velma's dropping off her Monday pies, a woman came in looking for cookies. It seems that the local bookstore is holding a book signing tomorrow and she wanted to provide refreshments. We chatted a bit and after some negotiation, she ordered five dozen cookies, which I am to deliver to the bookstore by nine a.m. tomorrow morning."

I picked up a cookie and took a bite. As expected, it was delicious. "Shortly after I moved to Holiday Bay, I walked past that bookstore and almost went in. I was feeling kind of down and my writing career wasn't back on track yet, so in the end, I decided that visiting a bookstore might just make me feel sadder, so I walked on by. I do remember that it was charming."

Georgia nodded. "Firehouse Books is really quaint and cozy. Did you know that the building in which it's located used to be an actual firehouse? There is still a fireman's pole in the center."

"I'll definitely have to check it out. Maybe I'll go with you when you deliver the cookies tomorrow."

"I think that meeting the local bookseller is a good idea because you will have a new book coming out in the near future."

I took another bite of the cookie. "The manuscript is finally back on track and almost finished, and in a few days it will be in Kate's capable hands, but there is no guarantee that it will be published anytime soon. Still, I do agree that it would be a good idea to get to know the local bookseller. She may even know of other authors living in the area. I used to belong to an authors' group back in San Francisco. I admit I missed a lot of the meetings, but it was nice to have men and women with a common interest to network with."

Georgia slid a cookie sheet out of the oven and set it on a cooling rack. "I totally think you should come with me tomorrow. And after we drop off the cookies, you can come with me to the community center for the Valentine's Ball committee meeting."

I frowned. "The ball is just a week from tomorrow, isn't it? I can't believe it is already February. Where did January go?"

Georgia smiled. "You've been working so hard on your novel that I'm not surprised you lost track of time. I'm glad you got your muse back."

"Yeah, me too." I glanced out the window. The snow was still falling, but it had slowed considerably. "I'm going to walk out to the road to get the mail. Do you think Ramos would like to go with me?"

Georgia glanced at her huge black dog. "Ramos is always up for a walk. Before you go, though, and before I forget to tell you, I spoke to the bride who inquired about having her wedding here in September and she is totally fine with a soft reservation for now."

I smiled. "That's great. Our first booking."

"And it's a big one. She wants to rent out all six suites for four nights, and to hold both the wedding and reception, as well as the rehearsal dinner, right here on the property."

I pulled on my jacket. "That's great. Did you discuss costs at all?"

Georgia shook her head. "I told her that if she wanted to send me a detailed description of what she wanted in terms of food and whatnot, we could come up with a price. If you ask me, after speaking to her, I didn't think the money it would cost would be an issue as long as we are able to provide the wedding she has been dreaming of."

"And did her dream seem reasonable?" While I would welcome such a large booking, I certainly didn't want to get involved with a bridezilla who couldn't be pleased no matter what we did.

"I think so. If we get to the point where we are ready to sign a contract, we'll just need to make sure that we ask all the right questions and that everything is spelled out in detail so there are no surprises." Georgia began stacking cooled cookies into boxes. "Don't worry. I've catered weddings before. That might not be the same as hosting the entire event, but I've learned along the way what sort of questions to ask up front to save tears and heartache down the road."

I decided to trust that Georgia knew what she was talking about. She was going to be the inn manager, so I should let her manage. I pulled on my hat, gloves, and heavy boots, called to Ramos, and headed out into the snow. Lonnie had been keeping the drive plowed for us, so the snow on the pavement was only an inch or so deep. I supposed once the remodel was complete and Lonnie wasn't coming over on an almost daily basis, I'd need to hire someone to do it. But that wouldn't be an issue until next winter, so I would just add *plow service* to the list of items to take care of at some future date.

Once I arrived at the box, I pulled out the stack of mail and slid it into the pocket of my jacket. The snow was beginning to pick up again, so I turned around and headed back to the cottage.

"Anything interesting?" Georgia asked when I walked in.

I pulled the pile of envelopes from my pocket. "Bill, trash, trash, bill," I said as I tossed each envelope onto the counter after glancing at the address of the sender. "Now here's something."

I set the envelope on the table, pulled off my hat and gloves and shoved them into my pockets, and took off my jacket and hung it on the coatrack by the door.

"Eleanor Quinn from Portland, Oregon?" Georgia asked.

"I think that Eleanor Quinn might live in the house that was once owned by Maddie Westmore." This seemed to confuse Georgia, so I elaborated. "I wrote to Maddie Westmore, Velma's aunt, who lived in Oregon, according to Charlee. I hoped if she was still alive and still lived in the same house, she might know Reggie's whereabouts."

Georgia frowned. "How did you get the address?"

"I found an address for Madeline Westmore of Portland, Oregon, while doing an online search, though it was connected to a document that was more than ten years old. I had no way of knowing if the woman still lived on the same property, or even if the Madeline Westmore I found was the Aunt Maddie that Charlee mentioned as being the woman who might know what had become of Reggie, but I figured it wouldn't hurt to send an inquiry and see what happened."

"And...?" Georgia asked.

"Let's find out." I ripped open the envelope and began to read. "'Dear Ms. Sullivan: My name is Eleanor Quinn. I am the daughter of Madeline Westmore and received the note that you sent to her. Mom is currently living in a long-term care facility.

She is in the final stages of dementia and I doubt she can help you in your quest. I do, however, believe that she knew the Reggie you are looking for. There is a photo on the bookshelf of two teenage girls. Mom told me they were her nieces, Velma and Regina. I never met either of them and can't say where either woman might be living now, but I did find a listing for Regina in one of my mother's old address books. I'm sure the address is at least a decade old, but I thought I'd send it to you anyway. Good luck in your attempt to reunite the sisters. Eleanor.'" I looked up at Georgia. "The address she provided is in Boston."

"So what are you going to do?" Georgia asked.

"I'm going to drop a note to Regina at this address to see what happens."

Georgia sat down across from me. "Does it mention her last name? If she married, it most likely isn't Upton anymore."

I frowned. "No. The address just provides the street number and name, city, state, and zip. I suppose I'll just send it to Regina Upton and see what happens. The worst thing that will happen is that the letter will be undeliverable and I will have to pick up a new trail."

Georgia placed a hand on my arm. "Are you sure you should be doing this without talking to Velma? She really might not appreciate your gesture. It could even ruin your relationship with her."

"If it looks like we have been able to track Reggie down, I'll talk to her. I don't want to mention what I am doing until I have something more. The reality is, tracking Reggie down at this point might not even be possible." I sat back in my chair. "How are you doing with your own mystery?"

"To be honest, I haven't had a lot of time to do much work on it. Were you able to set up an interview with Willa Baker? It seems that speaking to her about what she remembers about Victor and Ursula might give me a good place to jump in."

"I haven't spoken to her, but I will make the call right now. Maybe we can chat with her tomorrow while we are out. What time will the committee meeting you plan to attend be over?"

"By noon at the latest."

"Okay, I'll see if Willa can meet with us right after lunch."

I called Willa and set up an appointment to meet with her in her home at one o'clock the next day, then logged onto my computer to check my email. There was one from Kate, letting me know that she had spoken to my old publisher about my new novel. They were very interested in seeing the manuscript when it was done, and I emailed back to let her know that the manuscript was just about complete and I would be sending it off to her the following week.

There was also an email from one of Ben's old colleagues, asking if he had anything either on his personal computer or hard copy files that pertained to official investigations he was working on for the San Francisco Police Department at the time of his death. I emailed back to say I didn't think so, though I hadn't touched his computer since his death and, while he had left files behind in his home office, I hadn't had the heart to go through those either. I asked if there was something specific he was looking for. Since Ben had died more than a year ago, I had a feeling something must have come up very recently that had led the colleague to suddenly contact me.

I logged off, but not before checking my social media accounts. I hadn't posted to any of them since Ben and the baby died, although I did look to see what others did from time to time. As I scanned through photos of men and women I'd once considered good friends, I realized that people who once meant so much to me now seemed like nothing more than vague memories of another life.

I closed my computer and then answered my phone. "Hey, Colt. What's up?"

"Lily May," Colt answered. "She called me a while ago to tell me that she had something important to share about Karen's death. I told her that we could meet in my office or I could come to her home, but for some reason, she asked if you and I could meet with her at Velma's."

"Velma's is closed," I pointed out.

"I know. I said as much to Lily, but she told me that she was calling me from Velma's place, and it was Velma who'd suggested that we meet her there."

"Okay," I said, even though I had no idea why a woman I had never met wanted me to attend a meeting involving the death of another woman I had never met. I supposed it could have been Velma's suggestion. She had really appreciated the fact that I had been part of the team who found a young girl who had been kidnapped the previous fall. "When do you want to meet?"

"How about now?"

I glanced out the window at the snow. I supposed now that I lived where snow was a frequent occurrence, I couldn't use it as an excuse not to do things. "Okay. I'll be there in twenty minutes."

The road between the cottage and the restaurant was bad, but I somehow managed to make it without ending up in a ditch. When I arrived, I found Velma, Colt, and a young woman I imagined must be Lily sitting in a booth, talking.

Velma stood up, crossed the room, and poured me a cup of coffee. "Thank you for coming."

"I'm happy to help if I can."

"Abby, this is Lily; Lily, Abby," Velma added as I slid into the booth next to Colt. "Lily here has some news to share, and she wanted you both to be here for the telling."

I glanced at Colt. He shrugged. I smiled at the woman, who looked to be more than just a little bit nervous.

"Okay," Colt said. "We are both here, and we are listening."

Lily glanced at Velma, who offered a comforting smile.

Lily looked at Colt, then began. "After you came to speak to me about Karen's accident a few weeks ago, I had the idea to look through some of the boxes of mementos she'd left behind to see if I could come across any clues as to what she might have been upset about."

"Boxes of mementos?" Colt asked.

"Karen's cousin cleaned out her apartment and dropped some stuff that she thought Karen would want me to have. Mostly it was photos and scrapbooks and stuff. I was happy to have the reminders of my best friend, but the pain of losing her was too raw, so I just stacked the boxes in my closet. After we spoke, I decided to take a peek."

"And did you find something?" Colt asked.

"I'm not sure." Lily looked at me. "Do you believe in coincidences? I mean really random, far-fetched coincidences that are such a long shot that they seem to have no basis in reality?"

I frowned. "Yes. I guess. I once ran into an old neighbor from the block where I grew up while on vacation in Paris. I thought that was a pretty unlikely occurrence."

Lily let out a breath. "Yes, exactly like that." She paused and looked at Velma, then back at me. "I understand that before moving to Holiday Bay, you were married to a man named Ben Sullivan who died in an auto accident."

I nodded. "Yes, that is right."

"Do you mind if I ask where Ben went to college?"

I thought that was an odd question but didn't see the harm in answering. "UC Berkeley. We both attended. In fact, that was where we met. Is there a reason you asked?"

"When I was going through the boxes, I found a newspaper article about an off-duty homicide detective who was killed in a car accident with his infant son. I remembered Karen telling me about an old friend of her brother who had been killed in an accident. I remembered that it was someone she had known well at one time but hadn't seen for quite a while. I remember that she was really upset, and when I saw the article and the name, it sort of clicked."

My brows shot up. "You think Karen knew Ben? My Ben?" I almost screeched.

"Karen's older brother went to UC Berkeley. His name was Mark Stinson."

I gasped. "Ben's roommate was named Mark Stinson." I frowned. "But wait. I thought Karen was an only child who was raised by her mother after her father died."

"Mark was Karen's half brother," Lily explained. "They shared a father. When Karen was maybe seven or eight, Mark brought his roommate, Ben, home with him for the summer. They lived in Indiana at the time. Shortly after her father died, Karen and her mother moved to Holiday Bay."

"I do remember Ben mentioning his summer on a farm. The two of us got together the following spring." I took a moment to process what had turned out to be, indeed, a huge coincidence. "I can't believe that Karen knew Ben. I mean really, what are the odds?"

"Probably about the same as running into an old neighbor half a world away," Velma said.

I glanced back to Lily. "You told Colt that you had news about Karen's murder. Is there more to this story?"

"When was the last time you spoke to or communicated with Mark?" Lily asked.

"Wow, I don't know. It's been years. At least five. Why?"

"Did you know he was dead?"

I paled. "Dead?"

Chapter 9

Lily nodded. "I didn't figure this out until I spoke to Chief Wilder about Karen's mood before she died. I remember telling him that about four months before, she had been going through a rough patch. For reasons I still don't understand, she never told me what was wrong. She seemed to work through it, and then a couple of weeks before she went on her hike, her mood changed again. She told me that a relative had died and she believed it was the result of an unexpected, trickle-down effect. She never said who'd died or what she meant about the effect, and I didn't push because she didn't seem to want to talk about it, but when I went through Karen's things and found the article about the death of her half brother, it occurred to me it coincided with her dark mood four months before."

"What happened?" I asked.

"Mark was walking along a busy street in Philadelphia when a man pushed him into the street, where he was hit by a bus. He was critically injured and died in the ambulance on the way to the hospital."

"Oh God," I gasped. "I hadn't heard. Ben never said a word."

"Ben was already dead when it happened. Mark was killed last March."

"Did they catch the man who pushed him?"

Lily shook her head. "He got away in the commotion."

My gaze narrowed. "So Ben and Johnathan were killed when a distracted driver swerved into their lane, four months after that, Mark was killed after being pushed in front of a bus, and four months after *that*, Karen was killed in a slip and fall at the falls. There is no way all that is a coincidence."

Lily glanced at Colt, whose frown was even deeper than my own.

"I get that the odds of Abby's husband knowing Karen are astronomical," Colt began. "And I get that the odds of Ben Sullivan and Mark and Karen being killed in random accidents within an eight-month period are beyond comprehension. But if all three were murdered, which is where I sense this is going, why?"

"I don't know," Lily admitted. "I just thought the coincidences were too great not to mention."

Colt looked at me. "Any clue as to a possible link that could have led to all three deaths?"

I shook my head. "No. I have no idea how they could possibly be linked."

Velma took my hand in hers. "You told me that you moved to Holiday Bay after seeing an ad for the house on the bluff."

I nodded. "Yes. That's right."

"Where did you see the ad?" Velma asked.

"Someone sent me an email with a photo of the house and a description of the area. It sounded perfect, so I jumped on it."

"Do you know who sent you the email?" Velma asked.

I shook my head. "It was just spam that managed to get past my filter."

"Had you been looking for a new house or researching Maine?" Colt came into the questioning.

"No. The idea had never occurred to me until I saw the email." Suddenly it hit me. "You think I was brought here?"

No one spoke, but I could tell they were all thinking the same thing.

"Okay, wait," I said. "I know how it looks, but there is no way I was brought here. The fact that I decided to chuck my old life and start over again by rehabbing a house I had never seen in a town I had never heard of could not have been foreseen. I'm not really sure why I acted on the email when I read it, but doing so was very unlike me. There is no way anyone who knew me at all would suspect that I would follow through and buy the house."

"You were in pain and in need of a fresh start. The house on the bluff probably seemed perfect when you saw it," Velma said.

It *had* seemed perfect. In fact, it had seemed like the answer to an unvoiced prayer.

"For the purposes of this conversation, let's assume that your husband and the Stinsons were all murdered, and all by the same person," Colt said. "Again I ask, why?"

"Maybe we are dealing with one of those I-know-what-you-did-last-summer things," Velma said. "Maybe Abby's husband and Karen and her half brother all did or saw something they shouldn't have during the summer Ben Sullivan stayed out at the farm in Indiana."

"Even if that were true," Colt countered, "why now? Ben Sullivan visited the Stinson farm more than a decade ago. If he saw or did something there, why would the killer wait all these years to enact his revenge?"

"Maybe he was in prison," Lily speculated. "Maybe the reason he wanted revenge against the three of them was because they were responsible for putting him there. Maybe he got out just before running him off the road."

No one responded, but I thought her theory made sense.

"I'm going to need all Karen's boxes," Colt said.

"Yeah, sure," Lily replied. "You can swing by my place to pick them up when we are done here."

Colt looked at me. "Do you have items that belonged to your husband that are similar in nature to the ones of Karen's that were left with Lily? Photos and mementos?"

"There are some boxes in storage." I frowned. "You know, one of Ben's colleagues just emailed me looking for old case files that he may have had on his computer or in hard copy."

"Do you have any?" Colt asked.

"I have Ben's laptop and I boxed up everything in his office. Everything that's in storage is in San Francisco. I planned to have it all shipped here once I got settled, but I haven't gotten around to it yet."

"Is there someone you trust in San Francisco who could get hold of the boxes and overnight them to you?"

I thought of Annie. I trusted her, but would she do such a big favor for me if I asked? Ben and I had friends I'd left behind, but if someone who knew us was running around killing people, I had no idea who I could trust. "I do have someone I can ask. I don't know if she will do it, but I can ask. If she agrees, she won't have a key to the storage room, but I can send it to her, and she can overnight the boxes to me when she gets it."

"Okay," Colt said. "If that doesn't work out, let me know and I'll figure out something else."

"And in the meantime?" Velma asked. "Might Abby be in danger of some sort?"

Colt let out a long breath. "I don't know. If you are right and we are dealing with an I-know-what-you-did-last-summer scenario, she shouldn't be a target. But if it is something else…"

"Something else like what?" I asked.

Colt shrugged. "Maybe they had something. Or one of them did. Maybe your husband, or Karen, or her brother, found something that summer and the killer hoped to find it."

"If that were true, it would be illogical to kill them before they found what they were looking for," I pointed out.

Colt chuckled. "True. I guess I didn't think that one through." His smile faded. "You said that one of your husband's colleagues emailed you looking for something. Did he say what it was?"

"No," I answered. "He was vague."

"And what is this cop's name?"

"Frank Ribaldie."

"How well do you know him?" Colt asked.

"Not well at all. He worked out of the same office as Ben and I met him a few times, but I can't say that I really know anything about him."

"Have you answered the email?"

"I responded and admitted that I had Ben's computer, as well as the files from his office, but that I hadn't gone through any of them. I asked if there was something specific he was looking for."

"Has he answered?"

I pulled out my phone and opened the mail app. "No, not so far."

"If he does, let me know right away, but don't get back to him in any way. I'm going to do some digging to see what I can find out about him."

"And in the meantime?" Velma asked. "How are we going to keep Abby safe?"

"There is no reason to think I'm not safe," I said. "If something happened the summer Ben went to Indiana with Mark, I was not a part of it. I hadn't even met Ben yet."

"And still, here you are. In the town where Karen Stinson lived," Velma said.

"It probably would be a good idea to stay close to home," Colt said.

"For how long? A month? Two months? Six? At what point will we know that the danger, if there even is any, has passed?"

"I don't know," Colt admitted.

"Let's face it, if some guy wants me dead, he can kill me in my home as well as anywhere else. I will keep my eyes open and I will take extra precautions, though, like not hiking alone."

I could tell by Velma's tight lips that she was less than satisfied with my words, but Colt agreed that it would be hard to guard against a threat that was so vague.

"If anyone else from your husband's past contacts you, let me know right away," he said. "Day or night. I always have my cell with me."

"I will."

"And let's get those files from San Francisco right away. Who is this person you think might help?"

"My sister."

"Okay. Then if your sister can't do it for some reason, let me know. I'll fly out there myself and get the boxes if I need to."

I closed my eyes, tilted my head back, and let out a long groan. "This whole thing is just so absurd. Ben was run off the road by a distracted driver. How could that have been planned?"

"Was Ben driving a frequently traveled route at a usual time?"

"Yes," I said. "He was coming home from work. The only thing that was different that day was that he had our son in the car with him. He'd offered to pick him up from my sister's, who had babysat for me that afternoon, because her apartment was close to Ben's office."

"So if he drove the same route every day at about the same time, it would be possible for whoever was driving the car to approach from the opposite direction, keeping an eye out for him."

"I guess it would be possible, but the odds are astronomical that they would meet. Especially because Ben stopped to pick up Johnathan and so was actually driving the route at a slightly different time than usual."

"I suppose the killer could have put a tracker on your husband's car and found him that way," Colt offered.

I suppose it was possible it happened that way.

"In all fairness, you should tell Georgia what is going on because she's living with you, but let's none of us mention it to anyone else until we figure things out," Colt added.

"Do you think that Georgia could be in danger when she is with me?" I asked.

"Probably not, but it would be a good idea for both of you to keep your eyes open just in case."

Colt arranged to follow Lily home to pick up Karen's boxes and I headed home. I could see that Velma was worried and wished I could do or say something to alleviate her concern, but at this point I had nothing to give. I needed to try to call Annie to ask for her help, but the coward in me decided to start by filling Georgia in.

"Wow," she said. "It isn't often that I am at a total loss for words, but that's the best I can come up with right now."

"Yeah, I get it," I responded. "I was pretty tongue-tied myself at first."

"What are you going to do? How are you going to get the files from your storage locker? Is there anyone you trust enough to fetch them?"

I was going to share with Georgia that I planned to reach out to Annie, but on the spur of the moment, I found myself telling her that I was going to fly out to get them myself.

"You are going to San Francisco? When?"

"As soon as I can get a flight. I'll fly out, rent a car, pack everything up in the big old suitcase I have that is also in storage, and then take the next flight back. If I plan it right, I should be able to do the whole thing in twenty-four hours."

"Are you sure? That's a lot of flying."

I nodded. "I'm sure. I thought about calling Annie, but even if she answered, which is highly unlikely, there is no guarantee that she would do as I asked. And even if she did agree, she'd want to know why. If I explained, she'd just worry, and if I lied and she found out about it, it could further damage our relationship. Fetching what I need myself makes the most sense."

"Okay, then, I'm going with you," Georgia said.

I frowned. "You don't need to do that. It is going to be a really long day."

"I want to. You are going to need backup."

"What about Ramos?" I asked.

"I'll ask Nikki to watch him."

I looked toward the dining table, which was stacked high with cookie boxes. "And what about the cookies? I'm going to try to fly out tonight if possible. If not, tomorrow morning for sure."

"I'll have Nikki deliver them. I'll have to call to let the group know that I won't be able to make the Valentine's Ball committee meeting, but someone can fill me in later, and I'll need to call Willa and reschedule with her."

I hesitated. On one hand, it would be nice to have company on the long flight, but on the other, I didn't want to put Georgia in any danger if I didn't need to. Of course, she seemed like the sort of person who could take care of herself, and sorting through the stuff in the storage room would go faster with both of us working on it. Besides, looking through those things for the first time since Ben and Johnathan's deaths was going to be emotionally draining. It would help a lot to have a good friend there for support.

"Okay, if you are really sure."

Georgia nodded. "I am."

"Then I'll go online to find us flights."

"And I'll call Nikki to ask her to make the delivery and watch the kids while we are gone."

Chapter 10

"Abby, wake up."

I swatted at the insect touching my cheek to no avail.

"We're here," a voice that sounded like it was coming to me through a tunnel insisted.

I groaned and opened my eyes. "Georgia?"

"We've landed in San Francisco. We are about to debark."

I looked around at the people who had piled into the aisle to retrieve their carry-on baggage. Georgia and I hadn't brought any luggage because we were heading back to the East Coast later in the day. I rubbed the sleep from my eyes, unbuckled my seat belt, and felt around under the seat in front of me for my purse. I must have slept for hours. The last thing I remembered was getting settled in for the flight west, buying a whiskey on the rocks to try to calm my nerves, and pulling my sleep mask over my eyes in an attempt to get at least a few hours of shut-eye after having been awake for more than twenty-four hours. It appeared the whiskey had done its job.

"What time is it?" I asked.

"Nine twenty Pacific time," Georgia answered.

I frowned. "That can't be right."

"Don't forget, we picked up three hours along the way," Georgia reminded me.

Oh yeah. I guess my brain wasn't all the way awake yet.

"Our flight home leaves at six ten. We'll need to be back at the airport by four thirty at the latest."

"That should be plenty of time." I opened my purse and dug around for a Tic Tac or a piece of gum. "I've arranged for a car rental, so we won't have to rely on finding a taxi or calling for an Uber. The storage building is about a twenty-minute drive from the airport, assuming normal traffic. I thought we'd stop for breakfast on the way. We should be able to get what we need, return to the airport, check in, and have lunch well before we need to board."

"Sounds like a good plan. Do you think we should have brought something to pack the files in for the return trip?" Georgia asked.

"I have luggage in the room. I'm hoping we can get everything into two carry-on bags so we don't have to check anything. If there are more files than I remember, there's a sturdy bag that locks that I used for my last trip overseas. We can load that up and check it if we have to."

Georgia stood up as the row in front of us filed into the aisle. "Looks like we are next. Do you have everything?"

I held up my purse. "All set."

Once we cleared arrivals, we headed to the car rental area. Thankfully, my car was fueled up and waiting. We hurried out to the garage, claimed the midsize Ford I had selected, then drove toward the exit.

"Ramos and I did a lot of traveling after my husband died, but we never made it to San Francisco. I understand your desire to get back to Holiday Bay as soon as possible, especially given the situation, but I'd love to spend time here someday."

"It is a beautiful city," I said as I pulled onto the freeway. "I have some horrific memories associated with it, but some wonderful memories as well. Maybe one day we can come for a visit and I'll show you around."

"I'd like that."

"There is a good little coffee shop not far from the storage building. I thought we'd stop there first. They have good food and tend to be quick. There are better places in town, but I don't want to take the time to drive out of our way. I don't think that it will take us all that long to go through the stuff in the storage unit, but when I left San Francisco my mind was on escape, not organization should I need anything later. I'm not even sure I took the time to label the boxes as I loaded them, so it may take us longer than I have anticipated to sort through everything."

"I think we will have plenty of time, and I'm starving, so anything is fine for breakfast."

******

"Wow," Georgia said after I rolled up the garage-style door to the indoor storage unit I had rented. "There really is a lot of stuff in here."

I bit my lip as I looked at the mess. The room was piled from floor to ceiling with boxes and furniture. There wasn't even a path to walk. We were going to have to move the stuff from the front of the unit to get to the stuff in the back. "Yeah, it is even worse than I remembered. I guess it was a good thing we decided on a quick breakfast."

Georgia put her arm around my shoulders. "That is okay. We have plenty of time. We know we are looking for items from Ben's office. Files and a computer. We'll just peek in each box, and if it contains something other than files or a computer, we'll start a pile out here in the hallway. We can move everything back in before we leave."

I nodded. "Okay. Let's get started. But let's also keep an eye on the time. I don't want to miss our flight."

Sorting through items from my old life was a somber experience. I wasn't expecting the tears that trickled down my face when I came across the old ceramic lamp Ben and I had picked up at a swap meet or the sense of mourning that filled my soul when I found a box of mismatched plates that he and I had bought at a secondhand store after we'd rented our first apartment together. We'd later purchased nicer dishware, but I never could bring myself to get rid of the hodgepodge we'd pieced together that first year.

"I found the suitcases," Georgia said as she rolled out the first of two large, stackable cases.

"Great. Let's set them aside. The smaller ones that will work as carry-ons are nested inside." Now that we had moved a third of the items from the room into the hallway, I stood and scanned the rest. "I think the things from Ben's office might be back in that corner. I remember now using rubber tubs for them, and I see some tubs there. There is some furniture in the way, but if we shove it aside, we should be able to get to it. Help me with the sofa."

"Oh nice," Georgia said. "Are you thinking of using some of this stuff in the inn? I bet the sofa would work in the sitting area of one of the suites."

I paused. "I'm not sure what I am going to do with this stuff. I didn't think past putting it in here and heading east." I positioned the sofa against the opposite wall that we'd just cleared. "I guess I will need to make another trip here at some point to go through everything. I can't store it forever."

I crossed the room to see what was beneath a blanket that had been thrown over whatever was stacked behind the sofa. My heart stopped when I saw it was Johnathan's crib. Georgia laced her fingers through mine and gave my hand a squeeze.

"Do you want to take a break?" she asked.

I couldn't speak, so I just shook my head. She seemed to understand because she gently lifted one of the panels of the crib Ben and I had spent two months looking for and set it to the side.

"Ben and I had very different ideas of what sort of crib Johnathan should have," I whispered as Georgia came back for the second of four panels. "I had my heart set on a white antique crib that I had seen in a tiny shop downtown, while Ben was very firm that his son was going to have a manly crib made of dark wood with the logo of the San Francisco Giants painted on the headboard."

Georgia ran her hand over the soft brown wood of the antique Jenny Lind crib. "I see you found a compromise."

I nodded as a single tear streamed down my cheek. "After a lot of negotiation." I placed my hand on my heart. "Johnathan did have a San Francisco Giants comforter for his crib, but he also had a mobile with fairyland creatures I loved hanging over his head." I took a deep breath. "God, I miss him."

Georgia stopped what she was doing and hugged me. "I know, sweetie. And I know you will continue to miss him every day of your life."

She was right. I could move to the farthest reaches of the earth and start a dozen new lives, but nothing was going to keep me from longing for the piece of my soul that had died along with my husband and baby.

Once Georgia had cleared the crib, it was possible to squeeze through and reach the black and gray rubber tubs I'd packed the things from Ben's office into. I pushed one of the tubs toward Georgia, who pulled it into the center of the room. I repeated that exercise five times until all six tubs were in one place and still allowed us to move around.

I opened the lid of the first, which contained items from his desk: the photos he had sitting there, pens and pencils, paper clips, a stapler, and the other things you'd find on the average desktop.

Georgia picked up a framed photo and looked at it. "What a wonderful photo"

I nodded.

"You both look so happy."

I took the photo and looked at it. "We were happy. Very happy. The photo was taken shortly after we purchased our condo. We'd taken a drive down to the beach just to get out of the house. It was windy and cold, so the place was deserted, but we were young and happy and didn't care that our toes were turning blue. Ben, who liked to snap photos, brought his camera, so when another couple happened along, he asked them if they would take a picture of us. I remember that my face was frozen, which might account for the overly animated smile, but Ben was relaxed and happy and charming, and I never wanted the day to end."

"Wasn't Ben normally relaxed, happy, and charming?" Georgia asked.

I hugged the photo to my chest. "Not always. Ben was a good man, but he was also serious, with serious goals. He didn't take a lot of time off to play on the beach. That afternoon was special."

"Do you want to set the photo aside to bring back with us?"

I nodded. "I do." I slipped the photo into my purse.

The first tub didn't result in anything of value other than the photo, so we opened the second. That one and the third contained files. We didn't have time to go through them now, so we decided to bring them all with us and then sort through them at home. Another tub was filled with books, the fifth with the things Ben had on the office wall and shelves: certificates, trophies, and diplomas. The last tub held his laptop and printer. I figured we didn't need the printer, so we loaded the files and laptop into the two carry-ons, then began restacking the things from the hall back into the storage room.

"This looks like it was Ben's desk calendar," Georgia said. "I think we should take it. Is there room in that suitcase?"

"It's pretty full."

"I'll put it in my purse," Georgia offered.

"You know, Ben had an organizer that he carried around all the time, even after organizer apps became available on cell phones. He said he had spent years developing a system and wasn't interested in changing just because technology had advanced. Did you happen to see it? It was black leather and zipped around three sides. The cover was old. I think he'd had it since before college, so the corners were worn. He just got new pages for it every year."

Georgia put her hands on her hips. "I don't remember seeing it, but we didn't look through the tub with the books. I wonder if it could be in there."

"Maybe." I began lifting the corners of the tubs, looking for the right one. When I found it, I took off the lid and began stacking books on the floor. I emptied the entire tub but didn't find it.

"Do you think he had it with him at the time of the accident?" Georgia asked.

He probably did. He was, after all, coming home from work when the accident occurred. "Yes, I think he might have."

"Do you have the items from the car? The personal items that must have been returned to you after it was towed?"

Suddenly I felt nauseated. I sat down on the floor and lowered my head to my lap.

"Are you okay?" Georgia asked.

I nodded. "I just need a minute."

"Of course. I'm sorry. I shouldn't have brought up the car."

I took deep breaths to fight off the panic attack that I could feel coming on. What happened was horrific, but it was months ago. I needed to pull myself together. "There was a bag," I choked out. "I never opened it. I couldn't."

"I totally understand," Georgia said. It was then I noticed the tears streaming down her face. "I'm so sorry. I wasn't thinking."

I took a deep breath in, held it, and blew it out slowly. "No. It's okay. I think you are right. The organizer was most likely with Ben and was most likely returned in the bag with the other things in the car. If Ben was intentionally run off the road, the organizer, which was almost a journal of his life, might contain a clue." I took a moment and tried to remember. "The bag was dark blue. One of Ben's colleagues brought it to me. It was a duffel bag, and the person who brought it to me said it contained personal items from the car and Ben's desk at work."

Georgia walked toward the back of the room. "I'll look for it."

I went out into the hallway that linked the storage rooms in this section of the warehouse. I walked to the end of one row and down the next. I knew the organizer could hold an important clue, but that blue duffel was one thing I never wanted to see again. I walked around for a good twenty minutes, then returned to find that Georgia had moved all the furniture and boxes into the room and was ready to close it up.

"Did you find it?" I asked.

"I did. I packed it in one of the carry-on bags. The cover has blood on it, so I don't recommend that you try to deal with it now. We can look through everything when we get back to Holiday Bay."

I nodded, taking one last look at the room filled with everything in the world that was left from my life with Ben and Johnathan. Everything except my memories, that is. Those, I was sure, would live on for eternity.

Chapter 11

Georgia and I were both exhausted when we got home, so we left everything we had brought back with us in the suitcases and went to bed. By the time I woke the next day, it was well into the morning, and even though I had gotten an adequate amount of sleep, I was tempted to ignore the files that awaited me and pull the covers over my head. If not for the delicious scent of something baking, going back to sleep was most likely exactly what I would have done.

"Morning, Rufus," I said to the cat who had slept curled up on the pillow next to me. "I think it is time to get up."

Rufus yawned and stretched.

"I know it is tempting to hide out in here where memories I have worked hard to suppress can't find us, but it smells like Georgia has made cinnamon rolls."

Rufus rolled over and snuggled in close to me.

"Yes, I know that today is going to be tough. Going through Ben's computer, his files, and his organizer, is not something I am looking forward to." I cringed at the thought of the blood Georgia had mentioned. "But if someone intentionally caused the accident that killed him and Johnathan, we need to figure out who is responsible. I can't abide the idea that someone might get away with something so unimaginable."

Rufus butted his head up under my chin and began to purr. I buried my face in his soft fur, shed a few tears to hopefully get them out of the way, and went into the shower.

"Good morning. How are you feeling today?" Georgia asked as she handed me a cup of coffee when I joined her.

"Okay, I guess." I glanced at the files she had unpacked from the carry-ons and stacked on the dining table. I noticed that Ben's desk calendar was on one side, and the pages from his organizer, minus the bloody cover, was next to it. "It looks like we are ready to get to work."

"We are, but let's eat first. I made sausage and cinnamon rolls. I know they are your favorite."

"They are." I slid onto one of the barstools that lined the counter.

"I spoke to Colt," Georgia said. "I told him that we had everything we felt was important from Ben's office and planned to look through it all. He said he'd stop in later so we could catch up. He seemed impressed that we had flown all the way to San Francisco to gather everything."

"He offered to do that exact same thing himself," I pointed out.

Georgia slid a browned roll onto a plate. "True, but hunting up evidence is his job. He is, after all, the chief of police."

"If someone intentionally killed my husband and son, there is no way I am leaving things to the cops. If there is a clue in those files, we'll find it."

Georgia set a plate in front of me. "I'm with you every step of the way. I've cleared my calendar and I am all yours for as long as it takes."

"Thanks." I cut off a piece of the gooey roll. "I appreciate that." I glanced at the table. "I see that you extracted the organizer from the leather case."

She nodded. "I didn't think you needed to wake up to that. I saved it, though, just in case you wanted it for some reason. If you don't, I can get rid of it."

I hesitated. "Thanks. I'm not sure if I want it or not. For now, you are correct, I don't want to deal with such a vivid reminder of what occurred. At least not today."

After we finished eating, Georgia cleared up the dishes and I tackled Ben's desk calendar and organizer. I hoped if something odd had happened, I would notice an anomaly and recognize it as such. According to his desk calendar, on the day Ben died, he'd appeared in court at nine a.m., then had a meeting with the sister of the victim in his current murder case at eleven thirty. Testifying in court and meeting with the relatives of victims was part of his usual routine as a homicide detective, so I didn't see anything odd there. After his interview with the victim's sister, he had a lunch meeting with his old partner, who had since retired. According to the desk calendar, they were to meet at one o'clock at a coffee shop near the police station. There were a few other notes, including a reminder to pick Johnathan up from my sister's after work. I looked carefully at each entry, but nothing seemed out of the ordinary. I then checked his organizer for the same day, which duplicated his calendar in a way, but there was additional room for notes and even pockets for items such as receipts. I think that Ben's favorite part of the organizer was the goals section, which took up an entire space at the start of each year.

I noticed all the same meetings and reminders mentioned on the desk calendar in the organizer. There was also a note to pick up his blue suit at the cleaner's and a reminder to send his Aunt Violet flowers for her birthday. I paused as I read the scribbles in his handwriting. I never had picked up the suit or sent the flowers. Not that anyone would blame me, but still, I wondered what had become of the suit. Unfortunately, Ben's Aunt Violet had passed away the summer after Ben's death, so I'd never be able to get those flowers to her on his behalf.

"How can I help?" Georgia asked after finishing up in the kitchen and sitting down across from me.

"I'm not sure. I think I might have better luck with the desk calendar and the organizer, so why don't you start with the files?"

"Okay. What am I looking for?"

I had no idea. "Ben didn't keep files on all his cases at home. In fact, other than an occasional file on a tricky case he wanted to spend extra time with, he rarely brought work home with him. At least not work relating to open cases. He did like to mess around with cold cases as sort of a hobby."

"A hobby?"

I nodded. "He looked into unsolved cases and revisited all the information collected to see if he could find something the detective who originally investigated it had missed. If I had to guess, most if not all the files that were in his home office will relate to old cases. I guess if you see something that looks to have been current in November two years ago, set it aside. And, of course, if you see anything at all with Karen or Mark Stinson's name on it, or any files on crimes that took place in Indiana, set those aside."

"Okay. I'll do my best," Georgia said, opening the first file.

"By the way, when you spoke to Willa about postponing our meeting about the old resort, did you set a new date to meet?" I asked as I began to work my way backward through the desk calendar and organizer from the day he died.

"We agreed to tomorrow morning at eleven. If that isn't going to work for you, I can call her again. She was very understanding that our plans had changed, and intrigued by the fact that we had found letters dating back to the nineteen forties, so she had no problem rescheduling."

"Tomorrow should be fine," I answered. "Unless we pick up a clue here today and need to follow up on that instead."

"If we need to change the date for our get-together again, I can call her later," Georgia offered.

I paused at an entry reminding Ben to take supplies to Roxi. Who was Roxi and what supplies? I suddenly realized that there could be an unexpected downside to going through Ben's stuff. I knew in my heart Ben loved me and would never cheat on me, but after finding a single mysterious entry, I found that I was obsessed with finding out who Roxi was. I supposed I could call his old partner to ask him if he knew, but I was supposed to be keeping a low profile on things. Because I didn't know if Ben had been murdered, I didn't know if there was someone out there I shouldn't trust. And if there was someone I shouldn't trust, I had no idea who that might be. It was best to stay off the radar of whoever might be keeping an eye on a possible situation.

"What did you work out with the Valentine's Ball committee?" I asked, more to distract myself from Roxi than because I really cared.

"When I called to tell them that I had to go out of town unexpectedly and wouldn't be able to make the meeting, I also said I wasn't sure I would still be able to volunteer. They seemed fine with my showing up if I could but weren't worried about it if I couldn't." Georgia held up a file. "Here is a recent case. Or at least it was recent then."

I held out a hand and Georgia gave me the file. The case involved a man named Denver Woodford, who had been shot while getting cash at an ATM, and a witness identified only as Roxi, who had apparently seen the whole thing. I guess that answered the question of who Roxi was. I supposed she might have been staying in a safe house, the supplies Ben was to bring to her to see her through. The case of who killed Denver Woodford would most likely be resolved by now. I did wonder how it had all turned out and what had happened to Roxi, but that was a mystery I would need to look in to on another day. I set the file aside. It didn't appear that it was in any way related to his death or to the deaths of Mark and Karen Stinson.

"Do you think it is odd that no one from the precinct came by to collect Ben's files after he passed?" Georgia said.

"I never stopped to think about it. I'm not sure that anyone even knew he had the cold case files. As I recall, he would copy the files of cases he was interested in and work on them at home. He left the original files in the file room downtown, and I don't think he discussed his hobby with the other detectives he worked with, so it is possible that no one even knew he had them."

"You don't think that Ben asked his colleagues for help or input?" Georgia asked.

"Not on the cold case files. He looked at them the way a lot of people look at the Sunday crossword puzzle. They were puzzles for him to work on, almost as a means of relaxation. I know that might sound odd because real people had died, and their deaths had gone unpunished, but that was the way he looked at them." Now, though, I picked up the file that he must have been working on when he was killed and wondered about it. It would seem odd that no one had come looking for it unless it was simply a copy of the official file and he'd left the original at work.

I was about to make a comment about the Denver Woodford case when Georgia's phone rang. She looked at the caller ID, "I need to take this." She stood up. "I'll just be a minute."

Georgia got up and headed into her room. I heard her greet someone named Mitch before she closed the door, cutting off my ability to hear the conversation. Just because she was living with me, didn't mean she wasn't entitled to have conversations with men I didn't know, so I returned my attention to Ben's desk calendar and organizer. I hadn't realized the extent to which he had made notes about every aspect of his life. It could have been a coping mechanism if he was prone to being forgetful, but I didn't remember him as being forgetful in the least. Of course, if all the notes were any indication, he didn't need to remember much on his own.

"That was my friend Mitch," Georgia said after returning to the room.

"I don't think I remember you mentioning someone named Mitch."

"You wouldn't because I'm sure his name has never come up. I met him when I lived in Boston. He works for the city as a planner. He has access to property records, so I asked him to look up the address Eleanor Quinn gave you to see if he could verify current ownership. The house is now owned by a couple named Cole and Emily Williams, but he was able to find out that Regina Upton owned the house before the Williamses purchased it."

"So Reggie is still using the Upton name."

Georgia nodded. "It appears that way. At least as of ten years ago. I asked Mitch to look for property currently owned by Regina Upton and he just called to tell me that he'd found both a house and a business with deeds held by Regina Upton in Concord, New Hampshire."

I sat back in my chair. "That isn't all that far away from here. We could make a trip there once we get all this sorted out." I waved my hand over the table in front of me.

"We could. But should we? I really think we need to talk to Velma before we go any further."

I knew that Georgia was right, but I was worried that we'd get her all excited about finding her sister and then Reggie wouldn't want to see her. I thought of Annie. It had occurred to me to drive over to her place, ring the bell, offer her a sincere apology, and hope that she invited me in rather than slamming the door in my face when we were in San Francisco. I suppose part of the reason that I hadn't acted on that impulse was because we were short on time, but there was another reason: I really did suspect that my overture would be met with a door closed in my face.

"We have bigger fish to fry right now," I finally answered. "Let's put the search for Reggie on the back burner and revisit it when we have time to focus on all the angles. I take it you wrote down the addresses?"

Georgia held up a piece of paper. "I did."

"Okay, then. I doubt she'll be going anywhere in the next few weeks. Let's focus on this and then think about Reggie Upton again later. And Georgia— thanks for checking with your friend. I know that you have been conflicted about my search for Reggie from the beginning."

"I am conflicted. I don't want Velma to be hurt, but I also think that God put sisters together for a reason, and I believe that those paired by fate should find a way to share the lives they were meant to share."

"Very poetic and I agree. Maybe you are right. Maybe our next move is to talk to Velma." I picked up a file that was resting on the top of the pile. "For now, however, let's find out who killed my husband and son."

Georgia nodded. She returned her attention to the file she had been looking at before the call. "I'm with you a hundred percent, for however long it takes."

I looked down at the organizer in front of me. I'd gone back several months and nothing had popped. I was about to toss it aside in favor of the case files when something caught my eye.

"Ben was in Philadelphia," I said aloud.

"When?" Georgia asked.

"The last week in August prior to his death." I looked up. "He told me he was going to Bethesda. He told me that he had training of some sort."

"Are you sure he didn't go to Bethesda?" Georgia asked.

I shook my head, pulling out an airline stub. "This was in the pocket of his organizer for August. It is a round-trip ticket between San Francisco and Philadelphia. Mark died in Philadelphia. I wonder if Ben went to see him. And if he did, I wonder why he didn't mention it to me."

Chapter 12

"I pulled the accident report for both your husband and Mark Stinson," Colt informed me several hours later. "It does not appear that the two deaths were linked in any way."

"What makes you say that?" I asked. I glanced at Georgia, who sat on the sofa next to me with Rufus in her lap.

"According to witness statements gathered at the time of the accident that killed your husband and son, a woman with blond hair who appeared to be in her twenties driving a late-model Mercedes veered into oncoming traffic. Your husband swerved to avoid her, lost control of his car, and it flipped three times before it settled onto the shoulder of the road. Both your husband and son were dead at the scene."

I was sure I was going to throw up. I never had asked to see the incident report. I knew my family was dead and I was struggling to get through each day. Somehow the need to know all the details never had become an issue with me. In fact, I could distinctly remember not wanting to know so no images would enter my mind.

Georgia reached across the sofa cushion and took my hand in hers. "The woman didn't even stop?"

"She did not. The witnesses were more concerned with trying to help the victims of the rollover than tracking down the woman who caused the accident, so, unfortunately, no one even got a license plate number. The car was black, which is a common color, and while most agreed it was a Mercedes, the witnesses didn't agree on the year or exact model."

"I just assumed it was a male driver who caused it," I whispered. "I don't know why I assumed that, but I did."

"I would have assumed the same thing," Georgia said. "Generally speaking, men are much more reckless behind the wheel than women."

I noticed Colt's lips tighten, but he didn't argue.

"And Mark?" I asked. "Do we have a description of the person who pushed Mark?"

"Male. Tall. Over six feet, according to witnesses. Thin, with light-colored hair. He was wearing a baseball cap. Witnesses could not agree on a team, but apparently it was blue. He also had on dark glasses."

"So not the same person who ran Ben off the road."

Colt shook his head in answer.

I leaned my head back and tried to ward off the tears pooling in the corners of my eyes.

"It sounds to me as if the death of Abby's husband was truly an accident," Georgia said. "But that Mark Stinson's death was intentional. Do you think that perhaps Mark's and Karen's deaths could be connected?"

"I think they could very well be. Karen fell in July, which is a popular month for hikers in the area where the falls originate. After her fall, I put out a call for anyone who might have been hiking that day in the hope that someone had seen something. No one I spoke to had witnessed her fall, but I did find a few hikers who remembered passing her on the trail. Everyone I spoke to said she appeared to be alone. I asked about other hikers who had been seen nearby that day and got a variety of responses. Two or three people remembered seeing a tall man hiking alone, so I went back to speak to those witnesses again and was able to confirm that the man was probably around six feet two or three inches tall, with a thin, lanky frame, and blond hair."

"Sounds like the man who pushed Mark," I said.

He nodded. "The fact that a man fitting the description of the individual who pushed Mark in front of the bus also fits the description of a man hiking in the area on the day Karen died does not prove she was pushed, but it certainly points to that conclusion in my mind." Colt looked at me. "I'm sorry I wasn't able to let you know that it didn't look like Ben's death was linked with the deaths of the Stinsons before you went all the way to San Francisco."

"It's fine. It's not your fault. I should have let you know what we were doing." I narrowed my gaze. "It does sound as if Ben's accident really was caused by a distracted driver, but I found a ticket stub in his organizer for a flight to Philadelphia in August, just a few months before his death. Given the fact that Mark died in Philadelphia, I have to wonder if Ben went to see him for some reason."

Colt frowned. "He didn't tell you he was going to Philadelphia?"

I shook my head. "Ben told me he was going to Bethesda for training. I knew he and Mark were friends. If he wanted to visit Mark for some reason, all he would have had to do was tell me that was what he was doing. I don't understand why he chose to keep the trip from me."

"I'll look into it," Colt said. "I'll see if I can find out how long he stayed and what he did while he was there."

"Thank you. I appreciate that."

"Do you have old credit card statements from that period? Phone records?"

I shrugged. "Ben paid the bills, but I remember seeing a box with financial records in the storage unit. I didn't bring them back with me."

"It would be easy to get the records from the credit card and phone companies. I can request them, but it would be quicker and cleaner if you asked for them yourself."

I nodded. "I'll dig up the information today."

"What if Mark was in trouble of some sort?" Georgia asked. "Maybe he called his old college roommate who he knew was a detective and asked for his help. Maybe Ben didn't tell you about his meeting with Mark because he asked him not to."

"I suppose it could have happened that way," Colt said.

"Was Mark living in Philadelphia at the time of his death?" Georgia asked.

"No," Colt answered. I admit I assumed he had been and was surprised by the answer. "He lived in Baltimore. I'm not sure why he was in Philadelphia. I plan to look into it."

"Mark was married the last time Ben and I saw him," I said. "He and his wife, Sherry, were in Napa to go wine tasting and asked us to meet them for dinner. I guess that was maybe five years before Ben's death. In fact, it was just a few months before Ben and I decided to get married. Mark and Sherry were living in Los Angeles at the time, I think. Anyway, a year or so after that, Ben told me that Mark and Sherry had divorced and Mark had moved east. If he specified where on the East Coast, I don't remember. I never saw him again after Napa, and I didn't think that Ben had either, but now the trip to Philadelphia makes me wonder."

Colt looked at me. "You said that you found the ticket stub for Ben's trip to Philadelphia in a pocket in his organizer. Was there anything else there related to that trip?"

"I don't think so. I'll look again." I glanced at my phone. "If you'd like, I can pull up Ben's phone records and credit card receipts right now. We had online bill pay for both and I have the key with the passwords Ben set up."

"It might be helpful. If we can find out why Ben was in Philadelphia, we might be able to figure out what sort of trouble Mark may have been in, if that was what was going on. If he did ask for Ben's help, one of them must have kept notes of some sort."

I was certain Ben must have. He kept notes on everything. All I needed to do was find them.

Georgia took Ramos out for a walk while I pulled up the credit card and phone records Colt wanted, and he returned a few calls he had received while we were talking. I wasn't sure if I was disappointed or relieved that Ben's accident had most likely not been related to Mark's and Karen's deaths. I guess I was relieved that Ben wasn't wrapped up in something that had resulted in both his death and that of our son, but not having an identifiable person to go after meant that the person who caused their death would most likely never be held responsible.

The first thing I did was pull up the old credit card statements. I scanned through charges for airline tickets but did not find one for Philadelphia. I did find one for Bethesda, though, with a hotel charge during the same dates. Maybe he really had gone to training. I shuffled through the items I had set aside from that morning's search and found the airline ticket from his organizer. It was one-way, from San Francisco to Philadelphia, on the day before he would have left for Bethesda. I wondered if he hadn't simply made a stop in Philadelphia on his way to training. If he knew Mark was going to be there, that might have made sense even if there was nothing going on. They were, after all, good friends who hadn't seen each other for a number of years. The only question I had was why he wouldn't have told me that he was going to visit with Mark for a day or two on his way to his training. I also wondered how he'd paid for the airline ticket to Philadelphia if he hadn't used our joint credit card. And where had he stayed while in Philadelphia? The only hotel charge I saw was for the hotel in Bethesda.

"Is something wrong?" Colt asked when he finished returning his calls. "You are scowling at the screen."

"I found this ticket stub for a one-way flight in Ben's name from San Francisco to Philadelphia that coincided with his trip to Bethesda. Actually, this flight was dated one day before the round-trip ticket from California to Maryland. I suppose it's possible that Ben decided for whatever reason to make a detour, but I can't find where he changed his flight. The ticket stub I found wasn't charged to our joint credit card. I also didn't find a charge for a hotel in Philadelphia, although there was one for Bethesda."

"He might have just stayed with Mark. And Mark might even have paid for the airline ticket to Philadelphia. I'll see if I can find out how the flight was paid for. You keep looking for notes or additional receipts. We need to know what Mark and your husband were up to during that visit before his death."

I agreed with that, so I carefully made my way through Ben's organizer one day at a time. If there was a clue to be found, I was going to find it.

"How was your walk?" I asked Georgia a short time later, when she came in with Ramos.

"Wonderful. It is a beautiful day today. You should try to get outdoors for at least a short break. It's chilly, but the sun is out and the sea is gorgeous."

"I'll try to take a walk later."

"Any progress?" she asked as she took off her coat and hung it on the rack.

"Not really. It does look like Ben went to Philadelphia on his way to Bethesda, but I'm not sure how long he was there or whether he saw Mark. We are making that assumption based on the fact that

135

Mark was killed there, but so far we have zero proof of it." I leaned back in my chair. "I feel like we might be jumping to conclusions that aren't true to make sense of things. It's the same as with the boxes we found in the basement of the house. Yes, it was a huge coincidence that we found boxes that belonged to three girls who went to school together, were the same age, and were either dead or missing, so I understand why we came to the conclusion that the boxes were the link, but they weren't at all. When we found that Ben, Mark, and Karen, all people who knew each other going back years and died within a few months of one another, we assumed the deaths were related. But now it looks as if Ben's death at least is not related to the others. I found an airline ticket for Ben from San Francisco to Philadelphia and began working on the assumption he went to see Mark there, but he lived in Baltimore. We don't even know for sure that he was in Philadelphia at the time of Ben's visit."

"Actually, we do." Colt came in from the bedroom holding his phone. "I was able to get hold of Mark's credit card statement for that August. I didn't find airfare, but he probably drove from Baltimore to Philadelphia. I did find a charge for a room for three nights, beginning with the date of Ben's flight to Philadelphia. I called the hotel and confirmed that Mark rented a suite, and that there had been two men staying in it for the whole three-day period."

Okay, well, I guess that answered that question. If Ben had gone to Philadelphia to meet with Mark, he must have had a good reason. If he stayed for three days, it sounded as if he blew off the first two days of training. Why? He was serious about his career, so he must have had a really good reason. And even more importantly, why hadn't he told me about it?

Georgia made a fresh pot of coffee, then sat down at the table to continue with her perusal of the files we had brought back. Now that we knew that Ben's death had not been linked to the other deaths, I doubted she'd find anything, but it didn't hurt to keep looking. As I'd come to know, the clues that could blow a case wide open were often found in the most unlikely places.

"I'm going to head into the office," Colt said. "If you find anything, call or text. I have a few feelers out that I hope may give us some additional information. In the meantime, I have a thief to track down."

"A thief?" I asked.

"Four businesses in town have been hit in the past three weeks. Each one was robbed after they closed, and each one reported a loss of cash amounting to less than five hundred dollars. I don't think we necessarily have a criminal mastermind on the loose, but it is my job to track him or her down."

"Was the cash left in the register?" I asked.

"Each business had a wall safe, which is where the money was stolen from. Whoever is behind this knows how to crack a safe; that much is a given. All of the safes were opened, not destroyed."

"Sounds like a pro," Georgia said.

"In terms of talent, yes, but as I said, no business lost more than five hundred dollars. There was over two thousand dollars in one safe, but only four hundred and fifty-nine dollars was taken."

"Weird." I said.

"Very," Colt agreed.

Chapter 13

Willa Baker lived in a modest house about a mile from Holiday Bay's downtown area. It was not large, but her home was well maintained, and while the yard was covered with snow, I could tell by the dormant shrubs that it was probably spectacular during the spring and summer, when the flowers were blooming.

"Sure, I remember Ursula," Willa said after offering us seats at her kitchen table and pouring us each a cup of tea. "She stayed at the resort for an entire summer when I was eleven or twelve. She was a nice woman with sad eyes and what I imagine was a longing in her heart, who used to sit out by the pool late at night after everyone else had gone in for the evening."

"Is that how you met her?" Georgia asked. "Did you climb the fence and find her sitting there?"

Willa nodded. "At first I was afraid she was going to rat me out, but she said she wouldn't, and I really wanted a swim, so I stayed. We didn't chat that first night, or any of the next few nights after that. I'd find her sitting by the pool when I climbed over, and she would be sitting there looking up at the stars. I'd wave and she'd wave back. I'd swim and then leave."

"But you eventually spoke to her," I prodded.

"After a few weeks of maintaining a relationship based on a wave and an occasional hello, I arrived for my nightly swim to find her crying. I almost ignored her altogether, but I guess I had a tender heart even back then, so I approached her and asked if there was anything I could do. She said that she had a problem she needed to work out but that there wasn't anything I could do to help, so I went ahead and had my swim and left. After that evening, however, when I'd first arrive at the pool, I'd take a minute to sit with Ursula and ask her about her day. At some point, after we had been chatting for a few weeks, she told me that she had a secret that she hadn't shared with anyone. I told her I was good at keeping secrets, and she told me that she was pregnant."

"The gift," Georgia said.

Willa raised a brow.

"In the letters, Ursula talks about a gift that she had received from Victor. The letters are vague, and at first I thought the gift was something like a valuable piece of jewelry, but after a while I began to suspect that the gift was a baby."

"From what I knew, I would be willing to bet that you are right. I don't know everything that happened. I was just a child. But Ursula told me that she was pregnant and very scared. I asked about the baby's father, and she told me he was in the military and stationed overseas. I didn't ask for details and she didn't provide any. By the time I went back to school in September she was gone, and I didn't see her again until the following summer."

"And the baby?" Georgia asked.

"Ursula told me that the baby's father was killed overseas, and she arranged for the baby to be raised by a family. I don't know who she gave the baby to, but she said the family lived right here in Holiday Bay, the place, she confessed, that would forever hold her heart."

"That is so sad," Georgia said.

"Do you know the baby's name or the name of the family who adopted the baby?" I asked.

Willa shook her head. "Ursula never said. I was young and didn't really wonder, so I never pushed for an answer. She did give me something during the last summer she stayed here that might provide a clue if you are really interested."

"What's that?" I asked.

"Hang on." Willa got up and went down the hallway. When she returned, she showed us a photo of a child of about three or four standing in front of a white picket fence. She had brown curly hair, big brown eyes, and the biggest smile I had ever seen.

"Is this Ursula's daughter?"

"It is. The last summer Ursula came to Holiday Bay was when I was fifteen. She was thin and pale and looked awful. I asked her about it and she told me she was sick. She said she probably shouldn't have made the trip, but she had wanted to see her daughter one last time. She showed me the photo, and while she still didn't tell me her name, she confirmed that the child was her daughter. After she left, Mrs. Jasper from the spa gave me an envelope and told me that one of her guests had left it for me. The photo was inside."

"And Ursula?" Georgia swiped at a tear at the corner of her eye.

Willa shrugged. "I never saw her again. I guess she might have died. She must have been awful sick when she was here."

I took another look at the photo. "Do you know about how old the child in this photo is?"

"I guess she must have been born in 1949, so I suppose that at the time the photo was taken she was three."

"Do you have any idea where this fence was located?" I asked.

Willa shook her head. "It was just a fence."

"I wonder what happened to the baby," Georgia mused.

There didn't seem to be a way to find out, but I wondered the same thing. Willa allowed us to make a copy of the photo, then we thanked her and left.

"The little girl would be around seventy now," Georgia said after we had returned to my car. "I wonder if she still lives in Holiday Bay."

"It would be unlikely but not impossible. I suppose we could poke around a bit. Try to figure out who in town who is currently seventyish and might have been adopted."

"It's not a subject that will come up easily in general conversation."

"No," I admitted, "but we can talk to people we know who are close to that age. Charlee and Velma are a bit younger but have been here for a long time. They might recognize either the child or the fence."

Georgia shrugged. "It wouldn't hurt to ask. I am curious to see how this very sad story ended for the child."

"Yeah, me too," I said. "It sounds like the story of Ursula and Victor was more of a tragedy than a love story."

"I wonder who Harriet was and why they didn't want her to find out about the baby."

"We suspected that she was his wife, and even though he had gotten Ursula pregnant and was most likely overseas at the time the letters were written, Victor could still have been married to Harriet."

"I suppose." Georgia turned slightly so she was facing me. "I'm hungry. Do you want to stop in to show the photo to Velma? We can grab some soup or a sandwich while we are there."

"I could eat." I pulled the car over, executed a U-turn, and headed back toward town.

******

By the time we arrived, the lunch crowd was beginning to clear out and Velma was at the counter with a line of people waiting to pay their bills. She waved at us to grab a seat wherever, so we chose a booth by the window. As long as we were having a sunny day, I intended to enjoy it. I knew after living in Maine for only a few months that sunshine in winter was something that should not be taken for granted.

"Afternoon, girls. What can I get you?" Velma asked when she'd freed herself up.

"What is your soup and sandwich special?" I asked.

"Tomato soup and a grilled turkey and cheese sandwich."

"I'll have that," I said.

"Ditto," Georgia agreed.

"Coffee?" Velma asked.

We both replied that we would like coffee as well.

Once Velma had left to pass our order on to her cook, I pulled out my phone to check for messages. I didn't want to miss an update from Colt should he call or text with one. I was still interested in finding out whether Mark's and Karen's deaths were related, even if they had nothing to do with Ben's, and how Ben's trip to see Mark might be connected to them. I'd gone through Ben's desk calendar and organizer in great detail the previous day but hadn't found anything that shouted out that it was a clue.

"Still nothing?" Georgia asked.

"Not so far."

"I suppose these kinds of investigations take time. And Colt did have those burglaries to investigate as well."

I sighed. "Yeah. I know. I guess I just want to have everything wrapped up. The fact that Ben seemed to be involved has opened wounds that were finally beginning to heal."

Georgia put her hand over mine. "I get that. It's been a crazy couple of weeks, hasn't it?"

Velma set our food on the table, then pulled up a chair at the end of the booth. "So, what have the two of you been up to?"

I wondered where to start but decided to go with the child in the photo. I pulled up the photo I had taken with my phone and passed it to Velma. "I don't suppose you know who this child might be? The photo would have been taken in around 1952."

"That's some time ago." Velma frowned. "Where did you get this?"

"From Willa Baker."

Velma looked up. "Perhaps you'd better back up a bit."

I turned the floor over to Georgia; this particular mystery felt more like hers than mine. She was more connected emotionally than I was, or at least she had been. Now that I knew that both the mother and the father of the child seemed to have died early deaths, I felt a tugging at my heartstrings as well. I listened as Georgia spun the tale that began with the discovery of the letters in the wall, segued into her reading them and the connection she felt with them, and ended with our conversation with Willa and the details of Ursula's life that she'd shared.

"That is some story." Velma looked at the photo again. "I can't say that I know who this child is, but I do recognize the white picket fence."

Georgia's face brightened. "You do?"

"You know that big house up on the bluff that belongs to the Hamilton family?"

"Sure," Georgia answered.

"There is a fence with these little spade things on the top just like the ones in this photo around the rose garden in the back. I won't go so far as to say that it is the only fence ever built with this particular design, but it is pretty unique."

It was a unique design, I realized. "Do you think that Ursula gave her baby to a Hamilton?"

Velma paused to think about it. "The Hamilton house that stands now was built by Havilland

Hamilton back in the 1930s. He raised his three sons in it, and it was eventually passed down to Jasper Hamilton, who recently left it to his son Wesley."

"It just occurred to me that Jasper Hamilton, the man who founded the local bank, had the same first name as the man who owned the house when it was a resort," I said.

"It was a fairly common name back then," Velma informed us. "Anyway, I think that Jasper was around sixty when he passed, so if Ursula gave the baby to Havilland Hamilton, she would have been older than his oldest biological child."

"Do you remember there being an older child?" I asked.

Velma shook her head. "No. And just because the photo was taken in front of the fence does not mean that she lived in the home. She could have been the child of one of the household workers, or even of a neighbor or friend."

"I know that Jasper Hamilton is dead, but his wife, Patrice, is still alive," I said. "I wonder if she knows who the child is."

"I guess you could ask her. Wesley inherited both the bank and the house when his father passed, but Patrice still lives in the house. If you'd like, I can arrange for you to speak to her."

"Thanks, I'd appreciate that," Georgia said.

"Any news on Karen's death?" Velma asked.

I wasn't sure how much to share, but I knew I could trust Velma, so I eventually started at the beginning and brought her up-to-date.

"My, you have been busy," she said. "I can't believe you went all the way to San Francisco for just a few hours."

"It was a long day, but it worked out fine. I'm not sure anything we brought back will end up helping us solve this mystery, but we can hope."

Velma's expression softened. "This must be hard on you, going through everything all over again."

I nodded. "It has been hard. But if it helps, it will be worth it. I know how much I want justice for Ben and Johnathan, and I'm sure there are people who want the same thing for Mark and Karen."

"I know I would like to see justice served," Velma said, patting my hand. "If there is anything I can do to help out, you just let me know."

"I will." I glanced at Georgia. "I depend on you both to keep me sane, so the chances are better than average that I will come calling for help at some point. I don't know what I'd do without the family I have found here in Holiday Bay."

"We love you too, sweetie. Any more word from your sister?"

"Not so far. It has been a while since I have sent her one of my chatty emails. Maybe I will write another one this evening. I know it is up to me to try to pry a door open for us to rebuild our relationship, which is only fair because our estrangement was mostly my fault to begin with."

I couldn't help but notice the thoughtful expression that crossed Velma's face. Maybe she would be willing to walk through the door to her own reconciliation with her sister if Georgia and I were successful in finding it for her.

Chapter 14

In the end, Georgia and I made a last-minute decision to attend the Valentine's Ball as volunteers. I had a red dress that I had lugged all the way out from San Francisco but hadn't worn since I'd been living in Holiday Bay, and Georgia had found a darling pink strapless at a secondhand store in an after Christmas sale and had purchased for just this occasion. Because neither of us had been able to guarantee our attendance much in advance, we'd ended up assigned to cleanup at the end of the event. In the meantime, we were free to dance and mingle.

"Wow, the place is packed," I said to Georgia after we checked our coats.

"It does look like almost everyone in town has made it here. That is one of the things I love best about Holiday Bay: Everyone really commits."

Georgia had a point. Pretty much every resident I had met since moving here participated in the town-sponsored monthly events.

I waved to Lonnie and Lacy as they waltzed past. They looked so happy and so very much in love. I couldn't help getting choked up a bit when I noticed the look of complete contentment on Lonnie's face as he stared into the eyes of his wife.

"Champagne?" Tanner walked up with glasses for both Georgia and me.

"Thank you, kind sir." Georgia beamed.

I accepted the glass of bubbly and took a sip. It was actually very good. I wasn't expecting much, given that the champagne was included in the price of the ticket.

"Are you here with anyone?" Georgia asked.

"Nikki." Tanner looked around the room. "Of course, she dumped me the minute we walked through the door, so I was happy to see the two of you standing over here. I don't usually attend this dance, but Nikki badgered me into it."

"Well, I for one am glad she did." Georgia tipped her glass toward his.

Suddenly, I felt like a third wheel, so I made my excuses and hightailed it to a table where I saw Velma sitting with Charlee. I was happy to help out with the dance because it was an important fund-raiser for the town, but after everything that had gone on this past week, my nerves were much too raw for anything even remotely approaching romance.

"I wasn't sure you were going to make it." Velma pulled out a chair and indicated I should have a seat next to her.

"I wasn't sure either. In fact, Georgia and I didn't decide to come until this morning. We both think it is important to be an involved part of the community, and volunteering at these sorts of events is part of being involved."

Velma nodded toward the dance floor, where Georgia and Tanner were dancing cheek to cheek. "It looks like your roommate is making the most of her volunteer duty."

I smiled. It was good to see her having fun. "We are on the cleanup committee, so our volunteer duty hasn't even begun, but I agree that it is nice to see Georgia happy." I glanced back toward Velma. "And where, might I ask, is your date?"

"Right here." Charlee chuckled as she raised her hand.

I smiled in return. "I guess that works. I'm sure there are unattached men to dance with if you feel the urge."

"After being on my feet all day, sitting here chatting with Charlee is more my speed," Velma assured me.

"I think Colt plans to be here later if you feel the desire to take a twirl," Charlee offered.

I held up my champagne glass. "Thanks, but I'm good. Although I do have a few things I need to discuss with him. Did he say when he'd be here?"

"When I saw him earlier he said he needed to finish up his paperwork on the store burglaries and then he'd be by," Velma informed me.

"Did he catch whoever was doing it?" I asked.

Velma nodded her head. "He did. Although I don't think arresting the guy gave him the satisfaction that you'd think."

"And why is that?" I asked.

"The thief turned out to be a man with three young children who rolled into town on fumes and needed money to buy gas and provide food and shelter for them. I'm not suggesting that it was okay for him to steal from folks, but I do feel for him. In fact, if he had explained his situation to me, I would have given him the four hundred dollars and change he stole from me, saving him the trouble of breaking in."

I frowned. "I thought the thief was a professional burglar."

"Oh, he was. It seems the guy used to break into safes as a regular means of making a living, but then he met the mother of his children and decided to go straight. He got a job and lived as an upstanding citizen for almost ten years; then his wife got sick and the medical bills started piling up. After his wife died, he packed up his kids and headed out in his van. I think he had plans to find a place to settle, but he ran out of money, so he ended up reverting to his old ways."

I put my hand on my heart. "And what is going to happen to the kids?"

Velma shrugged. "Don't know. Colt called social services, and they're looking out for them while things get straightened out. I told Colt that knowing the man's story, I was not inclined to press charges, but five businesses in all were hit and there is no guarantee that all the folks robbed will feel that way. Even if all the victims of the burglaries agree not to press charges, Colt seems to think the guy will do time."

"Maybe someone can work out a plea deal for him," I suggested. "Maybe he can stay here in Holiday Bay so the kids can have some stability. If he can find a job, he can pay back what he took."

Velma looked at me with a soft expression. "That is one of the reasons I love you so. You have such a tender heart."

I took Velma's hand in mine. "You know I love you too." I glanced toward the dance floor. "I wonder if there is something we can do to help facilitate a compromise so that those kids won't end up in foster care. They did just lose their mother. I can't imagine how things would be for them to lose their father as well."

Velma squeezed my hand. "We'll talk to Colt about it when he gets here. It might take some wrangling to work out a deal that everyone can live with. I think I can convince the other merchants to go along with whatever we work out so long as Colt can be convinced to speak to the DA on the guy's behalf. I don't think the man has been arraigned yet, so we might be able to work out a deal before the DA even gets involved."

"Maybe we should confirm that the man is worthy of helping first," Charlee added. "We know the story he told Colt, but before we jump in and get involved, we should make sure it's authentic, not just a ploy to gain everyone's sympathy."

Charlee was right. It made sense to look at the guy's history. Still, I remembered that Colt had said he took less than five hundred dollars from each merchant, even when there was more than that in the safe. In my mind, that made him something of a gentleman thief.

The conversation segued into other topics, including the Easter parade and egg hunt in April. I was sharing the fact that we'd had a request to host a wedding in September when Georgia came over with Patrice Hamilton.

"I'm so happy that you were able to make it." Velma got up and hugged Patrice.

"I wasn't going to, but Wesley insisted that I come with him," Patrice said, referring to her son. "He thinks that I have retreated too far into myself since Jasper died and is concerned for my mental health. Apparently, I have been grieving longer than is socially acceptable."

"Now, don't you let anyone tell you how long it should take to grieve," Georgia said, pulling out a chair for Patrice. "It takes as long as it takes. Folks who haven't lost someone as integral to their life as a spouse or child might not understand that."

"Thank you." Patrice smiled at my perky roommate. I was certain the two had never met before, but they already seemed like the best of friends. Leave it to Georgia to make a new friend in under ten minutes.

"So where is Wesley?" Charlee asked.

"Dancing with his fiancée. He got me a drink and planted me at a table before abandoning me, but I was happy to see Tanner come over with Georgia."

"Where is Tanner?" I asked Georgia.

"He is at the bar, chatting with some friends. When I saw Patrice arrive, I figured it might be a good opportunity to ask her about our photo."

"And what photo is that?" Patrice asked.

I could see that Velma and Charlee were interested as well.

"Abby and I found some letters written between a woman named Ursula and a man named Victor. They were hidden between the wall and the built-in bookcase in the second-floor library in Abby's house," Georgia began. "After some research on our part, we were able to find out that Victor and Ursula had a baby while he was stationed overseas in the military. Ursula gave her baby to a local couple to raise, but we aren't sure who. The only clue we have is a photo of the child when she was about three. She appears to be standing in front of the fence that sections off your rose garden. We hoped you might know who the child is. We'd like to pass on the letters to her if we can find her."

"Do you have this photo with you?" Patrice asked.

I nodded. "On my phone, in my purse. Hang on and I'll grab it."

Georgia continued to fill Charlee and Patrice in on the background of the photo while I went to fetch my purse. I saw Colt walk in but decided to wait to connect with him until we had finished our conversation with Patrice. I returned to the table and pulled up the photo, then passed it to her.

"When was this taken?" Patrice asked.

"We think 1952 or thereabouts," I answered.

"I didn't marry Jasper until thirty years later." She frowned and looked closer. "This child would be older than he was when he passed."

"We think the child would be around seventy today," Georgia said.

"Bea Tiddle might know," Patrice said.

"Of course," Velma said. "I should have thought of her."

"Who is Bea Tiddle?" I asked.

"Bea used to work as a housekeeper for the Hamiltons. She is ninety-two now and lives with her nurse in a little house behind the big one on the grounds."

"I noticed that you had cabins on the property," I said.

"There are six houses that were built for full-time staff years back. Some lived there, while others chose to live in town."

"Are all the cabins occupied?" I wondered.

Patrice shook her head. "No. We have a vacancy now that the groundskeeper and his family left."

"I guess there isn't a lot of need for a gardener in the winter," I said.

"Oh, it wasn't that. The groundskeeper does see to the gardening, but he also shovels snow and takes care of the exterior of the house when it requires repair. The man left because he didn't get along with Wesley, who has been managing the estate since Jasper died. Before that, he had been with us for fourteen years."

"But Bea stayed even after she could no longer work?"

Patrice nodded. "She is like family. She has a hard time getting around now, but she is still sharp as a tack, and I know she began working for the family when she was around twenty, so she would have been around when that photo was taken. If you would like to come by to ask her about it, I can arrange for a visit."

"We'd like that very much," Georgia said. She looked at me. "Wouldn't we, Abby?"

"Absolutely. When would be a good time?"

"Bea doesn't get out much, so any day would probably be all right. She tends to tire by the end of the day and doesn't like to get up early, so maybe eleven o'clock?"

"How about the day after tomorrow at eleven?" Georgia asked. "That would be Monday."

"That should be fine. If you want to give me your number, I will confirm it with Bea and then call and let you know for sure."

Georgia jotted down her number and then dove straight into a conversation with Patrice about the history of her family and the bank. I wanted to chat with Colt, so I excused myself and headed in his direction.

"So, are you here alone?" I slid onto a barstool next to him.

Colt nodded. "I hoped you'd make it. Good turnout."

"It is a good turnout, which I suppose equates to a whole lot of cleanup later. Georgia and I are on the cleanup committee. At least I hope we are *on* the committee rather than *being* the committee. I'm not completely clear on that."

"As long as no emergencies pop up, I'll be happy to stay and help. Tanner mentioned something about hanging back to help as well. And I'm sure Nikki will stay if Tanner and Georgia do."

"That is very nice of you all and the help is appreciated. To be honest, I'm exhausted. I've enjoyed myself tonight, but I am beginning to wonder why I let Georgia drag me here."

"She does seem to have more energy than any two normal human beings combined."

"Which is why she is going to be the ideal manager for the inn," I pointed out. "I heard you caught your burglar."

Colt sighed. "Yeah, I got him."

"I heard the story. Is it true? About the kids and his wife?"

"It all seems to be true from what I have been able to confirm so far. Brady Baxter admitted to a life on the wrong side of the law when he was younger. He was never caught then, so he doesn't have a record, which is something when you think about it. He swore to me that after he met the woman he eventually married, he stopped burglarizing businesses and got a legit job, bringing home an actual paycheck. He worked hard, they bought a house, he coached his kids' sports teams, and his wife volunteered at their school. He and his one true love shared ten happy years and three children, and then she got sick. Cancer. He spent all the money they had and a whole lot of money they didn't have trying to save her. In the end, she died despite their effort. By then he was so far in debt there was no way out. He'd lost his job when he chose to stay home to take care of his wife during the last months of her life, and after she died, he packed his kids into his van and took off in search of a new start. He made it as far as Holiday Bay before he ran out of both gas and money. He was desperate to find a place to stay and to feed his kids, so he stole from the first business he was able to scope out. When the money from that theft ran out, he picked a second target."

"I feel for the guy, but it seems he was lacking a plan."

"Oh, he was. Baxter said he'd been looking for a job, but it is the slow season around here, so he wasn't having any luck. I feel for him too, but he really messed things up for himself and his kids."

"Yes, he did." I glanced toward Georgia and the others at the table. "So how can we help him?"

"Help him?"

"He didn't have a good plan, but he did end up here in Holiday Bay. It seems to me that this is the place to be if you need a second chance. How can we help him get his?"

Colt hesitated. "I don't know that we can help him. He broke the law. He is going to jail."

"Is jail the only outcome to this situation? Isn't there some other way? What if he gets a job and pays all the money back? Maybe he can do community service too."

Colt didn't answer right away, so I plowed forward. "Velma said she'd talk with the other merchants who were burglarized. She would be fine with a plan where he pays back the money instead of doing jail time and she thinks she can get the others to agree. If this father of three is basically a good guy who simply reverted to an old role after finding himself down on his luck, he might very well be worth saving. And those kids. My heart bleeds for them."

"The guy doesn't even have a place to live. I doubt we are going to convince anyone to return the children to him if he doesn't have a place to live and a way to support them."

"I have an idea. Give me a few minutes to see what I can work out."

I headed toward the table where Georgia, Patrice, Velma, and Charlee were still chatting. Patrice had an empty cabin, and it sounded like she needed a groundskeeper. I didn't know her, so I had no idea how flexible she'd be, but I figured it couldn't hurt to explain the situation and see if she would be willing to help.

Chapter 15

Once Velma, Georgia, and Charlee, got involved in the situation with Brady Baxter and his three children, I could see that seas would be parted if need be. Patrice was open to the idea of Baxter and his children moving into her empty cabin and his working for her family as a groundskeeper, so long as she could get Wesley on board. She admitted that he didn't always view the world in the same way she did, and his agreement to the plan was anything but guaranteed. In a way, it seemed odd to me that Patrice had so little control over the estate that her husband had owned, but she didn't seem to bemoan the situation, so I supposed his taking over was something that she was both expecting and comfortable with. In the end, it was decided that Colt would get involved to see if the concept we'd explored would be acceptable to everyone who needed to agree to it before Patrice wasted her time talking to her son.

Velma assured Colt that she could get the other affected business owners to go along with a plea deal if he and the DA were able to work one out. No one wanted to see three kids thrust into foster care if there was another answer. And it did seem that, while his actions were wrong, Baxter had done what he had for a good reason, although asking for help from a church or some other charitable organization might have been the better choice.

Charlee, who had worked for the local schools for most of her life and had connections with child protective services, agreed to meet with the right people to do her best to see that the kids were returned to their father if everything could be worked out. That wasn't guaranteed now that the agency was involved, but Charlee seemed to think that the people who worked for the agency were good people with a hard job to do who really wanted the best for the kids they represented.

Colt promised to work on the plan the group had come up with immediately, and I knew he would. He also seemed to want to find a solution that would allow Baxter and his kids to be together, and his confidence that he wasn't just stringing Colt along provided the confidence everyone else needed to tackle the problem.

In the meantime, Patrice had called Georgia to let her know that Bea was willing to meet with us on Monday if we liked. I never had gotten around to asking Colt about updates on the Mark Stinson murder case and hoped to get back to that today. I still didn't know why Ben had gone to Philadelphia to visit Mark, or whether their meeting had anything to do with Mark's and possibly Karen's death, but the answers I sought could wait one more day, if necessary, if it meant getting the mystery of Victor and Ursula's baby put to rest.

As promised, Colt had stayed around to help clean up after the Valentine's Ball, as had Tanner and Nikki. By that point in the evening, the conversation revolved around figuring out a way to help Brady Baxter and his kids. Tanner assured us that if Wesley wasn't on board with the groundskeeper job, he would hire the man to clean kennels at Peyton Academy. He didn't have a cabin to offer him to live in, but Tanner had a lot of money, and as long as the guy's story continued to check out, he would do whatever it took to help get him settled.

It really did seem, as I'd said, as if Holiday Bay existed to provide second chances. At least that had been my own experience. The people who lived here were truly exceptional and seemed to care about both longtime neighbors and those new to the town.

"Rufus slipped out when I opened the door to bring in the groceries," Georgia informed me when I emerged from my bedroom after working on a rough draft for a new novel that I'd been kicking around for a while. "He scooted under the front deck and won't come out. I've tried calling him, offering him food, even telling him we would go to Velma's if he came out, but he won't budge."

I reached for my coat. "I'll see what I can do. He slipped under the deck yesterday too, and it took me a good twenty minutes to get him out."

"There must be something under there that is attracting him. Maybe mice?"

I shrugged. "I suppose it could be something like that. He normally isn't one to want to spend time outdoors in the cold if an indoor option is available."

After I pulled on my boots, hat, and gloves, I went out into the cold. "Rufus. Here kitty, kitty."

"Meow."

It sounded like he was under my feet.

"Why don't you come on in and we can have a snack? It is freezing out here."

Rufus poked his head out from under the deck but did not come to me. "Meow," he said again.

"What has you so fascinated?"

It was then I heard another meow.

"Do you have a girlfriend down there?" I took a few steps toward Rufus, but he darted farther back under the deck. I knew that he had been altered, so I sort of doubted that a girlfriend was the reason for his odd behavior, but I'd distinctly heard a second cat. I got down on my belly and looked under the deck. It was dark, so I couldn't see much, but I could make out movement toward the back of the deck, where it met the house. I supposed that spot would be the warmest because the heat from inside would radiate outward.

"Come on, guys. Why don't both of you come out?"

Neither cat moved, and I was about to give up when I heard a tiny little squeak. A mouse? No, not a mouse. A kitten. "Are there kittens back there?"

Rufus meowed again but still didn't come forward. Making a decision, I headed into the cottage. "There is another cat under the deck, which I think is why Rufus is going under there. I think she has kittens. Either that or she is torturing a mouse. I heard a tiny little squeak."

Georgia's brows shot up. "Kittens? We need to bring them in."

"Yes, but how do we get to them? The cats are right up against the house. We can't crawl under the deck. There isn't enough room."

Georgia bit her lip. "I guess we can find something to use to pry up the boards and get them out that way."

I nodded. "I'm sure that Lonnie's crew left tools behind that will work. I'll run over and check."

Ultimately, we used a screwdriver to loosen the screws and a pry bar to leverage up the boards. The mama cat took off when we lifted them, but the three kittens she left behind were fully exposed. Georgia took them inside while I worked on catching Mom. It took me a can of tuna and a whole lot of patience, but eventually, we had the mother cat, her three kittens, and Rufus safely tucked inside the cottage. The mama cat almost panicked when she saw Ramos, so I laid down a plastic mat in my bedroom and used boxes to create a pen of sorts. I tossed a warm blanket over the top, then set bowls with cat food and water to the side. Once the mama and her babies were tucked in, I took Rufus with me back into the living room.

"We should put a cat box in there for the mother," Georgia suggested. "It might be risky to let her out. I'm afraid if she is freaked out enough, she might just take off."

"Yeah, that is a good idea. Rufus just goes out when he needs to, so we'll have to stop to pick up some supplies. I guess we can do that on our way back from our visit with Bea Tiddle." I glanced at the clock. "Which we should get to if we don't want to be late."

******

Bea Tiddle might not be as physically spry as she once was, but I had a feeling she was still as bright and alert as she'd been in her prime. After Patrice introduced us, Georgia explained about the letters, the photo, and the answers we hoped to find.

"Sure, I know who this is," Bea said.

I glanced at Georgia, who was grinning. "Do you mind sharing her identity with us?"

"What exactly do you want with her?" Bea asked.

"If she is the daughter of Victor and Ursula, and if she is still alive, we'd like to pass along the letters her parents wrote to each other," Georgia said.

Bea began to rock back and forth in her chair. "I see. I guess that she might like to have the letters. The girl in the photo was the daughter of the family who lived in the next house over years ago. Her name is Anabelle. Anabelle Winter. After she married, she was Anabelle Rosemont."

"Does she still live in Holiday Bay?" I asked.

"No. She moved away at least thirty years ago. We exchanged Christmas cards for a while, but it has been a few years since I last communicated with her. Maybe five or six, now that I think about it. The last address I have for her was in Hartford, Connecticut. I'd be willing to give you the information if you would like to try sending her a note. I can't say for certain that she still lives at the same address, but it is as good a place as any to start."

"And her parents?" I asked. "The couple who adopted her? Are they still alive?"

Bea shook her head. "Both are deceased. Anabelle's mama, Dotty, passed in 1997, and her father, Joe, passed in 2004. They were good people, both of them."

"Do you have any idea why Ursula chose them?" Georgia asked. "Did she know the couple she gave her baby to?"

"I'm not sure. I didn't know Ursula, but I did speak to Dotty and Joe on occasion. They shared with me that they had adopted a baby girl after trying for years to have a child of their own. I think they were happy. At least when they lived here they appeared to be. As I said, I never met Ursula, but I think she made a good choice when she decided who would raise her daughter."

I was happy to hear that. I could see that Georgia was as well. Even though we had never met anyone directly involved in this saga, I think we both felt we had a vested interest in it. We visited with Bea and Patrice a while longer and then left with the last address Bea had for Anabelle and a promise to let her know if we managed to track her down. While we were on the property, Patrice offered to show us the cabin that was currently unoccupied. It was a simple home but would be adequate for the Baxter family. There were three bedrooms, a modest kitchen, a single bath, and a small living room. There was a huge lawn on the grounds away from the formal gardens where Patrice said it would be fine for the children to play. I couldn't say for certain, but I suspected that Brady would be thrilled with the place should we be able to arrange for him to be released and his children to be returned to him.

"Do you want to grab a bite to eat before we head home?" I asked Georgia.

"If it's all the same to you, I think I'd rather just make us some lunch when we get back."

"That is fine with me. I know we have the makings for beef dip sandwiches."

"I was thinking that same thing. We should stop by the pet supply store to grab that cat box we talked about before we head out of town, however."

"That's a good idea. Do we need anything else? Dog or cat food?"

Georgia shook her head. "I think we are fine on both. I was thinking of inviting Tanner and Nikki over for dinner. Colt too, if he isn't busy. Would that work for you?"

I shrugged. "Fine by me. Why don't you call Tanner to see if he and Nikki are free? If they are, we can stop by the market after the pet supply store."

As it turned out, Tanner and Nikki were free and pleased to be invited over for some of Georgia's cooking, so I called Colt while Georgia ran into the pet store to get the cat box.

"Hey, Colt, it's Abby," I greeted when he picked up. "Tanner and Nikki are coming over for dinner this evening. Would you like to join us?"

"I'd like that quite a lot. That roommate of yours sure does know her way around the kitchen."

I chuckled. "Tell me about it. She is going to be famous when the inn opens and people get a taste of her slow-roasted prime rib. I think she's planning something simpler for tonight, though. She mentioned pork chops. We plan to eat at around six, so why don't you come by at about five?"

"Sounds good."

"Before you hang up, is there any word on either Mark's murder or Karen's fall? Anything new, I mean?"

"Not really. I am waiting for a call from a friend who might have additional insight into who might have pushed Mark in front of the bus, so I may have something to tell you by this evening. I don't suppose you found anything in your husband's notes that would explain why he went to see Mark before he went to his training in Maryland?"

"No. I haven't had time to go through everything more, but I'll keep looking. How are things going with Brady's case? Any chance the plan we hatched will actually work?"

"I ran the idea past a few people and I think it might fly. I am running an in-depth background check just to make sure there are no skeletons in his closet that we don't know about. If it comes out clean, I think we should be able to work out a deal that includes repaying the money he stole, community service, and probation in lieu of time behind bars. I spoke to my contact at child protective services who is open to the idea as well, as long as Brady has gainful employment and a place to live prior to the children being returned to him."

"Have you discussed all this with Brady?" I asked.

"I have, and he is, of course, all for anything that brings him back together with his children. He has held a variety of jobs in the past and seems like a handy guy. I think we should be able to work out the employment requirement."

"I took a look at the cabin on the Hamilton grounds just a short time ago. It has three bedrooms and a tiny but adequate kitchen and living area. I think that would work well. If the background check comes back clean and it looks as if the rest of the plan will be a go, she'll talk to her son."

"I hope to have a definite answer by tomorrow. If things come together the way I hope, this will be the last night Brady spends in jail, and his children will be out of foster care soon after that."

Chapter 16

By the time Wednesday rolled around, I felt that things were finally beginning to come together.

Georgia had written to Anabelle at the address Bea had given her. She explained who she was and why she was trying to get hold of her. She gave her both her snail mail address and her cell phone number, and Anabelle had called her just this morning, excited at the idea of receiving letters written by her birth parents. She was aware she was adopted but knew nothing about them other than the fact that they felt she would be better off with the loving couple who raised her. Georgia chatted with her for a full hour, ending the call with the promise to get the letters in the mail to her right away. We still didn't know who Harriet was, or why Victor didn't want her to know about the baby's existence, but maybe that wasn't really all that important.

Colt had received back all the information he was waiting for about Brady Baxter. Once he was able to confirm that Brady had a job, Colt was able to work out the plea deal and Brady was released from jail at the end of Tuesday afternoon. It had taken Colt a bit longer than he'd hoped, but the important thing was, he'd gotten it done. Patrice had somehow managed to talk her son into giving Brady a shot at the groundskeeper job, and he was moving into the cabin today. Someone from child protective services was going to do a site visit tomorrow, and as long as that went well, the children should be back with their father by the weekend.

The mama cat I had rescued was beginning to settle in, so I no longer had to keep her locked in the bedroom. She seemed content to have a warm, dry place to raise her babies, so I no longer feared she'd freak out and run away. I had no idea how Rufus had come to know there was a mama cat under the deck, but they certainly seemed like old friends. I didn't know a lot about Rufus's life before he came to live with me, but I was imagining they'd lived in the same household or at least had been neighbors at some time. I'd put flyers up in town, but so far, no one had claimed the mama cat as their own. Lonnie was hinting that if the owner wasn't found, he might surprise the kids with the adult cat once the babies had been weaned and rehomed.

"Is something wrong?" Georgia asked when she came in from walking Ramos.

I glanced up and frowned. "No. Why do you ask?"

Georgia pulled off her gloves. "You were scowling at your computer as I walked in. Have you started another manuscript?"

I leaned back in my chair. "No. It's not that. I was just checking my email."

"Was there bad news?" Georgia hung up her coat.

"More like no news. I've sent four emails to Annie since she sent me that short email on Ben's birthday, but she hasn't answered any of them. I knew that reestablishing a relationship with her would probably take time, but I hoped that the one email she sent was a sign that a door had been opened." I clicked off my computer. "I guess not."

Georgia sat down across from me. "I'm sorry. I know how hard this has been for you."

I crossed my arms over my chest. "Yeah. It has been tough, but I'm fine. I have endured disappointments and heartbreak in the past and have somehow managed to survive them, and I will survive this as well. My situation with Annie and the total frustration I have experienced regarding it has caused me to reevaluate things with Velma, though. When I first thought about finding her sister, I was coming off the high of having received that one email from Annie. Now that I have had the chance to revisit the bitter side of the fence, I realize that you were right all along. There is no guarantee that my looking for Reggie won't simply anger Velma. She mentioned that Reggie has known where she is all this time, and if she wanted to mend fences she knew right where to look. If we told Velma about Reggie and Reggie rejected her, that could really hurt her, which was never my intention."

"So what are you saying?"

"I'm saying that I think I should sit tight on what we know for now. If in the future the opportunity arises for me to provide Velma with her sister's current whereabouts, I can tell her what we know. In the meantime, I am going to leave it alone."

"I do think that would be best. But if the opportunity does present itself, you should definitely tell her what we know."

I stood up and walked into the kitchen. "Okay, so we are in agreement. We will file the address your friend dug up for another day."

"What are your plans for today?" Georgia asked.

"I am going to work on Ben's files. I still think that he may have left behind a clue about why he went to see Mark and didn't tell me about it. I still think that if I can answer that question, it could give us some insight into who might have pushed Mark in front of the bus. In my mind, solving Mark's murder is the first step in finding out what really happened to Karen, providing, of course, that she didn't fall after all."

"Do you need help?" Georgia asked.

I poured myself a cup of coffee. "I appreciate the offer, but I think that I would be more likely to recognize a clue if there is one."

"I'm sure you're right. I wanted to help if I could, but I had no idea what I was looking for the other day. I'm fairly sure that even if I found something important, I wouldn't recognize it as such."

I walked across the room and sat down on the sofa and Rufus climbed onto my lap. "I agree that I am more likely to notice any inconsistencies in Ben's notes, and I am fine going through the files on my own. Besides, isn't today the day you told me you were going to help Nikki with arts and crafts at the preschool?"

Georgia nodded. "Yes, that is today, and I really should keep my commitment to Nikki, but helping you when I can is always going to be my first priority."

"I'm fine. Go have fun with the kids."

Georgia got up from the table, crossed the room, hugged me, and then went into her bedroom to get ready. I ran my hands through Rufus's fur as I glanced at the files that we'd stacked in one corner of the room. Today was the day, I decided, I was going to find the message that I felt in my heart Ben had left for me to find.

I grabbed the stack of files closest to the top and set them on the table. I chose the first file in the stack and opened the cover. The file was for a cold case relating to an unsolved murder that took place in San Francisco in 1991. Three woman had gone out barhopping on a Friday night, and all three had ended up with their throats slit. The women were all found in different parts of town, but the medical examiner had determined that they were all killed within a few hours of one another and, most likely, by the same person. The killer had never been found. I didn't see what that could possibly have had to do with either Stinson, so I set that file aside and picked up the next one. It too was a cold case murder that had left the San Francisco police department stumped. After that I found files relating to a kidnapping, a mass shooting, and a series of arson fires that resulted in seven deaths. None of the files looked to me to pertain in any way to Mark or Karen, so I set that stack aside and grabbed the next handful of files.

In a way, I guess it did seem odd that Ben would spend time working on these cases. Most of them had been opened in the nineties and all had hit dead ends. As a homicide detective, he was knee deep in current homicide investigations all day, every day, so why had he wanted to spend his free time digging around in cases that had nothing to do with him?

I had been working for about ninety minutes when I came across a file that stood out as being different from the others. This murder had occurred fifteen years earlier. The unique thing about it was that while, so far, the other cases Ben had been digging around in had all originated in San Francisco; this file dealt with an incident that had taken place in a small town in Indiana. "Indiana," I said aloud. This couldn't be a coincidence. I quickly did the math and realized that the murder covered in the file could very well have occurred when Ben was in Indiana visiting Mark and his family for the summer.

I pulled out the summary report and began to read. Isaac Dumbarton was found shot to death in his home in July 2004. A neighbor, Mark Stinson, found him dead on the floor when he went by to return a chainsaw he had borrowed. My heart began to beat faster as I read. Mark Stinson! He would have been around twenty, and Karen seven at the time of the incident.

I continued to look through the file. Isaac's daughter, Isabella, had been staying with her father for the summer. The Dumbartons were divorced and the custody arrangement had Isabella living with her mother during the school year and her father during the summer. Isabella's mother was initially considered a suspect in the death of her ex; the divorce was a messy one, and she had fought hard for full custody with no scheduled visitation with her ex-husband. According to the report, Isabella was visiting a friend at the time of the murder, but the name of that child wasn't mentioned.

If Ben had been visiting Mark when the murder occurred, it made sense that he would be interested in resolving the matter, but why hadn't he ever mentioned it to me or told me he was going to see Mark? I still didn't know whether the reason he went to see Mark shortly before his death had anything to do with this cold case. Still, considering the location of the murder and the timeline, a case could be made for thinking that Ben had found out something about it, that his research had led him to Philadelphia all these years later.

The file Ben had amassed on the Dumbarton murder was the thickest of all the ones he had been working on. There were supplemental reports, photos, copies of interviews, witness statements, and, of course, pages and pages of notes that had been made during the course of the investigation. Toward the back of the file, I found an additional incident report, this one involving the death of a senior citizen who'd been run down and killed while crossing a street. The hit-and-run had not been witnessed and as of the time the report was made, the guilty party had not been found.

I put my hand to my chest. Another hit-and-run incident came just a bit too close to home. I took a deep breath, blew it out slowly, and willed my heart rate to slow. Once I had my emotions under control, I went back through the file and looked at every single piece of paper in it. The fact that Mark had been the one to find this man's body and then ended up being killed himself didn't seem to be a direct, causal relationship given the years between the events, but given the fact that Ben had been looking in to the matter, I was willing to bet a causal relationship was what we would eventually find.

I read every word on every page in the file, looking for a clue of any sort. It seemed to me that the most logical explanation for Ben meeting with Mark was that he had discovered something. Perhaps something that no one else had found. Not being familiar with the family or the case, it was likely that I might not notice what Ben had, even if it was right in front of my face to see. Still, I felt that I needed to try. I was halfway through my second pass when I saw a notation in the margin of one of the reports. It appeared to be a date and it looked to have been written by Ben: "7/18." The hit-and-run had occurred in June and the Dumbarton murder in July, but according to the police report it was on the tenth, not the eighteenth of that month. Something else could have occurred on the eighteenth that stood out to Ben. But what? And how on earth would I recognize the significance of whatever it was even if I stumbled across it?

I decided to start over again a third time from the beginning and read through every single piece of paper in the file, keeping an eye out for that date. It was eight days after the murder, so the investigation would have been well underway. It was more likely than not that I would come across a lot of references to that date. The trick would be in knowing what Ben had seen that had caused him to make a note of it. Of course, Ben had jotted down a month and a day but not a year, so I didn't know for certain that he was referring to July in the same year as the murder.

As I read and reread the file, I began to get a feel for the overall situation. Isaac Dumbarton was a local farmer who married Trish Newman, a graphic designer from Chicago. She was passing through town when her car broke down, Isaac helped her, and seven months later they married. Trish moved to Indiana and sixteen months after they wed, the couple welcomed a daughter into the world. When Isabella was five, Trish decided that farm life was not for her. She divorced Isaac and took Isabella to Chicago, where she resumed her career. Trish tried to win full physical custody of Isabella, but the judge awarded the parents joint custody, with court-ordered visitation for Isaac. According to witness statements, the relationship between Isabella's parents continued to deteriorate. When Isaac was shot and killed, there were a lot of folks who assumed that Trish was responsible because she just happened to be in town visiting friends at the time.

While there was a lot of information in the file, I didn't see any mentions of anything happening on July 18. Maybe the date meant something to Ben. Maybe when he reviewed the file he was reminded of something. Or maybe…

I grabbed the organizer and turned to July 18 of the year that Ben died. In the notes section of that page, there was a single word scribbled in Ben's familiar scrawl. *Denton.* In my mind, Denton must be a name. I tried to remember if that name had come up anywhere in the file I had just gone through several times, but I didn't think so. Still, it felt important. I realized it was just as likely that Denton was someone he was to meet on a case he'd been working on that

July and had nothing to do with the murder all those years earlier. I wondered how I could find out.

I picked up my phone and called Colt. "I might have found something that may be related to whatever could have been going on with Mark's and Karen's deaths."

"Sounds promising. What is it?" Colt asked.

"It's sort of complicated. Would it be okay if I came to your office?"

"I am on my way out for an interview. I can stop by your place when I am done. I shouldn't be more than an hour."

"An hour would be fine." I paused. "Does the name Denton mean anything to you?"

"I've been doing some digging and I'm pretty sure that someone named Theo Denton is responsible for both Mark and Karen's deaths."

Chapter 17

The hour that I had to wait felt like a lifetime after Colt dropped that piece of news and then rang off. I was pretty sure I was going to strangle him when he finally showed up. To pass the time, I went over to the house to check in with Lonnie rather than wearing a hole in the flooring with my pacing.

"The place looks great," I said as I stepped into the mostly complete first floor.

"I think it is coming together just right. I spoke to Bobby this morning and he confirmed that he will be here to start taking care of the mantel in the living room and the crown molding in the dining area a week from today."

"That's great. I can't wait to see how it all comes out. I have to say this project has been messier and noisier than I ever imagined, but it's also a lot of fun. I feel like the house has a new look every time I wander over."

"At this point there is something new to explore every few days. Georgia told me that you solved the mystery of the letters in the library."

"We did. And I suppose it turned out to have a happy ending. It is sad that both Victor and Ursula died so young, but their daughter lived on and had a happy life."

"I guess that's something. The flooring for the second story is going to be delivered tomorrow. We aren't quite ready for it, so I am going to have them stack it in the living room. I wanted to warn you in case you came over and wondered about it."

"Thanks for the warning. Did the guy with the cabinets get back to you?"

Lonnie nodded. "They should be in by the middle of next week. Things are really humming along. I hate to jinx it, but right now we are actually ahead of schedule."

"That's great. I don't want to jinx it either, so I will forgo the high five." I paused at the sound of a car in the drive. "That must be Colt. I'll check back in with you before the weekend."

"We'll be taking off at noon on Friday, but I'll make sure we chat before I go. Lacy has been talking about organizing a dinner party for Sunday, so I'm sure you'll hear from her later today. She is going to make some of her famous ribs, so if you are free it will be worth your while to come over."

"Dinner sounds fun, and I love ribs. If I don't hear from her, I'll call her tomorrow."

I waved to Lonnie and headed out the back door, which led out to the drive. "Okay, what is this about a man named Theo Denton killing Mark and Karen?" I asked before Colt had even managed to make it all the way out of his car.

"Isaac Dumbarton had a son from a high school fling with the prom queen, Sandra Denton. While Sandra and Isaac never got married and Sandra retained full legal and physical custody of Theo, Sandra continued to live in town, and Theo and Isaac were tight. By the time Isaac was killed, Theo was seventeen." Colt pulled something out of his jacket pocket and handed it to me. It was a photo of a tall, thin, blond man. "This is Theo Denton. Do you think we could continue this conversation inside?"

"Oh, yeah, sure. Sorry. I just got so impatient waiting for you." I started walking toward the front door of the cottage. "This guy fits the description of the man who pushed Mark."

Colt stomped the snow off his feet, then took a step into the entry. "He does and there is more." Colt took off his jacket and hung it on the rack. I hung my jacket up beside it. "Can I possibly get a cup of coffee?"

"Oh sure," I answered, heading to the kitchen. "So about Theo... Are you sure he killed Mark and Karen?"

"Sure, no. But mostly certain." Colt sat down on the sofa. I handed him his coffee, he took a sip, then set the mug on the coffee table in front of him. He pulled another photo out of his pocket before he spoke again. "I called everyone I had spoken to who had seen Karen on the trail the day she died. One of the witnesses had taken a bunch of photos, and I asked to see them. This was one of them."

The photo was of three people, two men and a woman. Walking behind them at the exact moment the photo was snapped was a man who looked an awful lot like Theo Denton. "Wow. That does look like him. If we can prove that this is Theo, I guess that would demonstrate that he was in the same woods as Karen on the day she fell to her death."

"I agree. Which is why I called a buddy of mine who works for the DA in Philadelphia and asked him if he could arrange to show Theo's photo to the witness who claimed to have seen a tall, thin man with blond hair push Mark in front of the bus. He was willing, and the witness told my buddy that there was an eighty percent chance that the man he saw push Mark was the same man. Unfortunately, the man who pushed Mark was wearing a baseball cap and dark glasses, so a hundred percent identity verification is probably not in the cards, even if we can find another witness."

I sat on the edge of the chair across from Colt. "Okay, say Theo killed Mark and Karen. Why?"

"That I don't know. I do, however, intend to keep digging until I find out."

"Do we know where he is now?"

"His last known address was in Philadelphia. He no longer lives there, but he did when Ben and Mark visited and when Mark died."

"So Ben and Mark must have gone to Philadelphia to talk to him, or to confront him. Maybe Ben found out that he had something to do with his father's death."

"Maybe. All we can do is speculate now, but we'll figure it out."

"If Theo did kill Mark and Karen, and he was living in Philadelphia when Ben saw Mark in Philadelphia, it tracks that Ben was aware of whatever was going on between Theo and the Stinsons. I still feel like there might be clues in his notes and possessions. I'll keep looking. I know it looks like Ben's accident had nothing to do with this, but it still feels like he was somehow involved in it."

Colt nodded. "If nothing else, he knew something."

"What about the boxes that Karen's cousin left with Lily? Did you find anything that might lead to a clue as to what was going on in Karen's life at the time of her death?"

Colt blew out a breath. "I opened the boxes and took a quick peek, but I haven't had time to look at every photo or read every letter. I suppose there could be a clue to be found."

"Are the boxes at your house or your office?"

"My home."

I stood up. "Okay. Let's head over there now and look. I'll help you, which will make the search go twice as fast."

Colt hesitated.

"You do want to figure this out, don't you?" I asked.

"I do."

"So let's figure it out. You know you can trust me not to blab any secrets I may come across while looking through Karen's mementos. Did she have a journal of some sort? A lot of people keep them."

"Not that I saw, but like I said, I've been busy and haven't taken the time to really sort through the stuff. You are correct, though; it is time to button up this case." Colt stood up. "Let's go. If we both work on it, we should be able to look at everything I have in a few hours."

******

Colt lived in an apartment in a small complex. It was barren and drab and not at all the sort of place where I would want to spend much time. Colt was single and he had a demanding job, so he most likely spent very little time in the cramped space. I could definitely see why he didn't think it was an adequate place to have his niece and nephew come for a visit. His idea to buy a home with a yard seemed like an even better one now that I had gotten a look at his current residence.

"Let's each take a box and go through it," Colt suggested. "There are eight in all."

I picked up a box, took off the lid, and began sorting through photos. Most of them looked as if they were of Karen in recent years and I doubted they'd hold a clue to her relationship with Theo Denton, but I didn't want to miss anything, so I took the time to look at each one and to see if there was any writing on the back. The box Colt selected for himself had yearbooks and scrapbooks. He appeared to be taking the same care as I as he went through each item one at a time.

"A lot of these photos are of scenery," I said. "There are a few with people in them, but most are of animals and landscapes."

"Karen liked to hike and ski. She spent her free time in nature and tended to do a lot of it alone." Colt held up a yearbook. "According to her high school yearbook, she was popular. I found photos that show that she was not only a member of the student council but was on both the track team and the girls' basketball team, and she was a member of the yearbook committee and a photographer for the school paper."

"I suppose that her desire to spend time in solitude could have developed after high school." I set the box I had been looking through aside and started on the next one. "If there is anything important to find in these boxes, it seems like it would be from her childhood. Something from her time in Indiana, because her link to Theo Denton is from Indiana."

"Unless she stayed in touch with someone even after she moved," Colt pointed out. "There could be a letter that might provide a clue."

I picked up a stack of letters between Karen and a man named Ron. They weren't all that old, so they probably didn't have anything to do with Theo or her and Mark's deaths, but I decided to take a peek anyway. I felt a bit like a voyeur. "Do you think that whatever Ben found during his investigation led to Mark and Karen's deaths?" I asked after determining that Ron was a past lover and setting the letters aside.

"It does look as if that might be the case, but until we find actual facts, I think we need to keep an open mind."

I picked up a diary, opened the cover, and began to read, but it appeared to be from her high school years, so I set that aside too. I suspected that if there was a clue to be found, it would be from a diary or journal during the last year of her life or her childhood before she moved to Holiday Bay. I picked up a newer-looking journal and began to read. My breath caught in my throat when I realized the last entry was written on the day that Karen died. "I think I have something."

Colt looked at me. "What is it?"

"Karen's journal. She wrote something in it the day she died."

Colt held out a hand. I passed it to him.

Colt began to read out loud. "'Some secrets are meant to be shared, while others are best taken to the grave. I have a secret that at one time I felt justified in keeping, but after finding out what actually happened to Mark, I am no longer certain that the pact Isabella and I made is one I should continue to maintain. I need time to think. Time alone to think over everything. I need time to work up the courage I know I will need to do what I know needs to be done.'"

Colt stopped reading.

"Is that it?"

He nodded.

"We need to work our way back. Maybe at some point she reveals what the secret that she feels burdened by is."

"Perhaps," Colt said. "But if the secret is one that is so heavy as to cause her this amount of angst, I'm not sure she would reveal it, even in a diary."

"She hints that what happened to Mark is in some way related to the secret," I said. "Lily said Karen mentioned to her that she was upset because of the death of a loved one and talked about a trickle-down effect. Karen seemed to be getting over the death until a couple of weeks before her own death. Perhaps when Mark died, she wasn't aware that it was connected to her secret. Maybe she had mourned the loss of her half brother but had begun to move on, but then she was made aware of that connection. Maybe she even felt a certain amount of responsibility for his death."

Colt leaned forward on his elbows. "Karen had a secret that in some way must have been related to Theo Denton. She'd kept it for all these years, but then Mark was pushed in front of a bus and Karen realized that it was Theo who pushed him, and he did it because of the secret she'd kept."

I nodded.

"So what was the secret?"

I paused to think about things a bit. "We know that Theo was Isaac's illegitimate son from a high school fling. They were close, despite the fact that Isaac never married Theo's mother. We know that Isaac was shot to death and that Isabella's mother was a suspect but was never charged. It appears that the murder occurred during the summer when my husband was in Indiana, visiting Mark. According to the case file, the Dumbartons were the Stinsons' neighbors, and Karen mentions Isabella in her journal entry, so the two of them must have known each other, maybe even were friends."

"So far I am with you."

"Years after Isaac's death, Ben goes to Philadelphia to see Mark there, even though he lives in Baltimore. It appears as if Theo lived in Philadelphia at that time, so I am going to assume that he was the reason for the visit there. We don't know what occurred in Philadelphia, but Ben died three months later in what appears to be an unrelated accident. Mark was pushed in front of a bus seven months after the visit by a man who fits Theo's description. Four months after Mark's death, Karen died in a fall, and it appears that it may have been

Theo who caused the fall as well." I looked Colt in the eye. "Whatever happened, it must have had something to do with Isaac Dumbarton's murder all those years ago."

Colt got up, crossed the room to the kitchen, took out a bag of coffee, and began to fill the coffeemaker. "What if Theo was the one who killed his father? What if somehow Mark and Karen knew it? Maybe Ben knew as well. Maybe they promised never to tell, but Mark changed his mind for some reason and Theo had to eliminate him."

I picked up a pen and began to click it open and closed. "Okay, say that is true. Why would they keep Theo's secret all that time? And if they did for some reason vow to keep his secret, why would he kill them more than a decade later? We can speculate that Mark changed his mind and was going to tell, but why would he?"

Colt poured two cups of coffee and set them on the table. "Yeah, that theory feels pretty weak. Still, I do feel like the murder is related, given the fact that it appears that Theo killed both Mark and Karen."

I bit my lower lip. "It just doesn't make sense that Mark and Karen would have been protecting Theo all this time. Maybe Karen wasn't protecting Theo. Maybe she was protecting someone else."

"Like who?"

"I don't know. Let's look around some more. Read more of the diary. Maybe Karen spells it all out somewhere else."

Colt picked up the diary he'd been looking at and I continued to search in the box. I really hoped Karen had written down her secret, but after hours of looking, the only conclusion I could come to was that she hadn't.

Chapter 18

It wasn't until the following day, when I was looking through Ben's things, that I finally figured out what must have happened. Or at least that was what I suspected. I called Colt and asked him to come over.

"I know what happened. At least I think I do," I said.

Colt sat down. "I'm listening."

"I found an interview Ben did a few months before he died. It was a human-interest piece that resulted from a case he had worked on in which a woman killed her abusive husband by poisoning him over time. The reporter asked Ben if he considered turning his back and letting the women walk because her reason for killing him was that he had practically broken every bone in her body, and Ben replied that while he felt compassion for her and what she'd been through, the murder clearly was premeditated, rather than an act of self-defense, and he felt she could have and should have found another way to deal with him. The reporter then asked Ben if he had ever been faced with a situation in which he was forced to choose between his responsibility to his job and his responsibility to humanity, and he said that he had not had to struggle between his legal obligations and his personal feelings since he had been a cop, but that he had been forced to make a similar choice in the past and, in the long run, it hadn't worked out for him."

"Did you know what he meant?" Colt asked.

"Not at first. But then I remembered a story Ben told me a very long time ago. He'd changed the names and some other identifying facts, but maybe a year after he made detective, he was handed a case in which a seventeen-year-old boy was shot and killed. He followed the clues and eventually found that the victim's neighbor, a ten-year-old boy, had been the one to pull the trigger after he found out that the gunshot victim had tried to rape his twelve-year-old sister. Ben was really torn up when he found out that the killer he had been looking for was a ten-year-old who was just trying to protect his sister. I made a comment about the unlikelihood that the killer would be a child, and how it would be impossible to prepare for such a thing, and Ben responded that he knew of a case in which a seven-year-old girl shot and killed someone in a similar circumstance."

Colt frowned. "So you think Isabella killed Isaac Dumbarton?"

"Maybe. I found notes that indicated that while Isaac had managed to talk a judge into ordering visitation during the summer, he took out his anger toward his ex-wife on Isabella, and there were reports of both verbal and physical abuse. What if Isaac had a gun and Isabella used it to protect herself? What if Karen knew what had happened and vowed to keep Isabella's secret, but over a decade later, Ben looked into things and uncovered a hornet's nest?"

Colt didn't answer right away. I could tell he was reviewing things in his head. "Okay. Let's assume for a moment that Isabella shot and killed Dumbarton. I seem to remember that he was killed with his own gun, which makes this scenario more likely. Why would Mark and Ben go to Philadelphia to confront Theo if Isabella was the shooter?"

"I don't know," I admitted. "I see there are a few holes in my theory. Even if Isabella shot Isaac and then told Karen about it, it doesn't explain how Theo fits in to it. I guess he might know that Isabella killed Isaac, and he then killed Mark and Karen to protect her secret, but that doesn't make sense either. Things work better if Theo is the shooter, but that doesn't fit with Ben's story about the seven-year-old unless he was referring to a different girl altogether."

"It seems that all the people who might know what actually happened are dead," Colt mused.

"Isabella isn't dead. Do we know where she is now?"

"No, but I'll see if I can track her down."

After Colt left, I took Ramos for a walk along the bluff. My theory that Isabella was Isaac's killer made sense to me, but it didn't explain why Theo killed Mark and Karen, unless they both knew what Isabella had done and had helped her to cover it up. It was Mark who found Isaac's body when he went over to his house to return a saw, but what if that wasn't what had happened at all? What if Mark said he found the body on the floor and no one else was home to cover for Isabella? Was it possible that after over a decade Theo found out about the cover up and was out for revenge? But how had he? And why had Ben and Mark gone to see him in Philadelphia, if that was what they'd done?

It was possible that Theo had found out what had happened and was threatening to go to the police. Perhaps Ben and Mark had gone to Philadelphia to talk him out of it. I guess if that was what had happened, the conversation must have taken a bad turn. But it was months later when Theo pushed Mark in front of the bus. Why had he waited so long, and what was Mark doing in Philadelphia again? Had Mark been there for another reason?

Turning to Mark and Karen's murder, there was another scenario that made more sense. It had Theo killing Isaac, and Ben figuring that out when he took a second look at the case. Maybe Mark and Ben went to Philadelphia to try to track Theo down but had been unsuccessful. Then Ben died in a terrible accident and could no longer help with the investigation. Maybe Mark went back to Philadelphia for a second look, Theo found out Mark was looking for him, and he pushed him in front of a bus. That still didn't explain why he killed Karen too, unless he suspected that Mark had told her he was the shooter and he was afraid that she'd go to the police.

Of course, that didn't explain Karen's secret. Unless Karen knew Theo had killed Isaac all along and hadn't told anyone, including Mark, who found out later from Ben, who figured it out based on the available clues.

I was starting to get a major headache. Eventually, I decided the only thing that made sense to do at this point was to wait to see if Colt was able to track down Isabella.

By the time I got back to the cottage, Georgia was home. "How were the arts and crafts?"

"So much fun." Georgia beamed. "I wasn't sure how it would go with so many kids to try to organize, but Nikki was really good with the kids, who seemed to adore her. They did whatever she asked them to do and everything went smoothly. Did you and Ramos have a nice walk?"

"Cold but nice. I've enjoyed the snow, but now I think I am ready for some warmer weather."

Georgia opened the refrigerator and began taking out ingredients for dinner. "I agree; some warm weather would be welcome. I think we have a couple more months of cold, however. I ran into Velma while I was out and she mentioned that we are supposed to get more snow over the weekend. Probably not a major storm, but it will be cold nonetheless. Do you remember where we put the jar of olives we bought?"

"I think they might be in the cupboard above the refrigerator. We could use more storage in this kitchen with all the cooking you do."

"Maybe we can figure out a way to add a pantry," Georgia suggested. "We can ask Lonnie for ideas."

"Speaking of Lonnie, he told me that Lacy wants us to come to dinner on Sunday. She's making ribs."

"Sounds good to me. I'll call her to see if we can bring something to contribute. I have a really good recipe for honey baked beans. I made a pot and took them over to Tanner's a while back and he said they were the best he'd ever had."

I smiled. I was sure Georgia's beans were to die for, but I was equally certain that Tanner would have gone all gaga over anything Georgia brought over, even if it was a pot of soapy water. The man was about as smitten as I'd ever seen anyone. Although Georgia didn't seem to notice. At least she didn't admit to noticing. I suspected she had a clue as to how Tanner felt about her. Either that or love really was blind.

Chapter 19

After a restless night, I woke at three a.m. and a seemingly unimportant clue that I had come across and discarded suddenly seemed like the most important clue of all. I turned on my bedside lamp and tiptoed out to the dining table where I'd left Ben's files. I grabbed the one covering Isaac Dumbarton's death and took it back into the bedroom with me. Then I clicked on the gas fire and propped pillows behind me, opened the file to the back, and took out the incident report on the hit and run. On June 19 of the same year that Isaac Dumbarton was shot on July 10, an elderly man was hit by a moving vehicle and left for dead. The person driving the vehicle was never found, and based on what I could tell, the case was never solved.

We suspected that Isabella might have shot Isaac in self-defense and that Karen knew about it, which was the secret she referred to in her diary, but what if the secret Karen kept was completely different? We knew that Isaac lived near the Stinson farm and we suspected that Karen and Isabella were friends. What if Theo, at seventeen, had been the one to run down the old man and leave him to die, and Karen and Isabella were in the car with him when it happened? It made sense that if Theo had caused the death of a pedestrian and did not plan to accept responsibility, he would have had to convince the girls not to tell either. If that was the secret Karen had kept, it could make sense for Theo to kill Mark to protect it if he somehow found out. It likewise made sense that he might have killed Karen if he felt she was going to back out on the pact she had made all those years ago.

So how did this tie in with the death of Isaac Dumbarton? Because my gut told me that both things did tie together. Isaac might have found out what Theo had done. Maybe he noticed damage to his car. Isaac might even have threatened to go to the police. Of course, in this scenario, it would make more sense if it had been Theo who had shot Isaac. But what if Isabella was home and Isaac went ballistic when he found out what Theo had done? What if things had gotten violent and Isabella had picked up the gun and threatened to use it if Isaac didn't stop beating Theo? Maybe the gun went off and Isaac was killed. Now there would be two secrets to keep: that Theo had killed the elderly man and that Isabella had killed Isaac. Theo might even have used the fact that Isabella had killed Isaac to cement the promise Isabella and Karen had made not to tell what Theo had done. He, in turn, would have agreed not to tell what Isabella had done.

This theory had a lot of ifs involved, but I felt that at least I had come up with a series of events that made sense. I hoped that Colt would find Isabella and we could confirm what we thought we knew once and for all.

Chapter 20

"The ribs were delicious," I said to Lacy after everyone assembled had downed each and every one of them, along with the baked beans and potato salad Georgia had brought and the green salad and rolls Nikki had contributed.

"The recipe has been handed down in my family for five generations. The secret is to start off with good-quality ribs and then cook them slowly. I usually do these in the summer when we can sit out on the deck, but I had a midwinter craving that could not be denied."

"Well, I am up for your doing ribs again when the weather warms up a bit. In fact, if outdoor seating is an option, we can have the meal at my place," I offered.

Lacy smiled. "I'd love that. Your view has to be the best in the area."

"Is there something I can do to help with the dessert?" I asked.

"No. I made a cobbler. I just need to heat it up. I'm going to check on the kids before I bake it. Hopefully, Colt will be here in time to eat the plate of food I set aside for him and then join us for dessert."

I glanced at the clock. "He should be here soon. I'll text him to see if I can get an estimate on his time of arrival."

Colt had been able to track down Isabella and had gone to talk to her in person. I was anxious to see how close we were with the two theories we'd worked out, assuming that she'd agreed to come clean. Colt texted back to let me know that he was less than a minute away, so I grabbed my jacket and headed out to the drive to meet him. Nikki and Georgia were in the den playing a game with the older kids, and Tanner and Lonnie were in the garage looking at the car he was restoring, so when Lacy had headed upstairs to check on the baby, I'd been left alone in the kitchen. I figured no one would miss me for a few minutes.

Colt pulled up and I slipped into the passenger seat. "How did it go?"

"It went fine, considering."

"Were we close? Did Theo kill the pedestrian and then make Karen and Isabella swear not to tell?"

Colt nodded. "That much was spot-on, with the addition of the fact that Theo was drunk when he hit the man who was in a legal crosswalk. I wish I knew how Ben figured it out all those years later. It was a brilliant piece of detective work, but he didn't leave adequate notes to explain how he did it."

I couldn't help but smile. "My Ben was a smart man and an excellent detective. I'm not surprised in the least that he figured out that Theo hit the pedestrian while Isabella and Karen were in the car and then made them swear not to tell. I imagine that after he figured it out he told Mark, and then Mark and Ben went to Philadelphia to confront Theo, but he wasn't around?"

"Theo was around, and when they confronted him about the hit and run, he told them that it was Karen who shot his father and he had proof. He said if they ratted him out, he would rat Karen out, so they left without reporting anything to the police. I guess Ben's death shook Mark up quite a bit. He tried to talk to Theo again to get him to confess to the hit and run, but instead of confessing, he pushed Mark in front of a bus."

"Wait. Karen shot Isaac? Why?"

"Isaac figured out that Theo was responsible for the hit and run and confronted him. Theo's response to the accusation was not to be remorseful but to mouth off to Isaac. That sent Isaac over the edge. He grabbed a bat and started hitting Theo with it. Isabella came in with Karen and tried to intercede on her half brother's behalf. Isaac shoved Isabella, causing her to fall into a table and hit her head. Isaac went back to hitting Theo with the bat, so Karen picked up a gun that was sitting on the table and aimed it at Isaac. She screamed at Isaac to stop, and somehow the gun went off and Isaac was shot."

"Why was there a loaded gun on the table in the first place?" I asked.

"Isabella wasn't sure, but she suspected that Theo had been target shooting when he was called into the house by his father."

"And after Isaac was shot?" I asked.

"Theo convinced Isabella and Karen to forget everything they knew. They wiped the prints off the gun, put it back on the table, and then Theo drove them over to another friend's house where they all spent the night. Mark found the body the next day."

"So Theo, Isabella, and Karen kept not one but two secrets for over a decade, and then Ben decided to dig around in an old murder case and found something that blew everything wide open. How very tragic."

Colt nodded. "It was tragic. Mark was an innocent bystander and Karen was a child who found herself in an awful situation. There is an all-points bulletin out for Theo, and Isabella has been put into protective custody until he is caught. She is the only one alive, other than Theo, who knows what really happened."

I glanced back toward the house. "Thank you for helping me get my answers."

"They were my answers to find as well."

"Are you ready to go in and have some ribs?"

Colt nodded. "I have been thinking about those ribs all day."

I opened the passenger door and got out. "We've eaten, but we saved you a plate. Lacy has cobbler for dessert too, so you'll want to save some room for that."

Colt fell into step beside me. "All I've eaten the past two days is fast food, so I have plenty of room for whatever she serves up. But before we leave the subject of Karen's death altogether, did you ever find the email you received that caused you to come to Holiday Bay?"

I opened the back door and stepped into the kitchen. "No. I didn't look for it. I might even have deleted it. Why do you ask?"

Colt peeled off his jacket. "I've been thinking about what Velma said about Ben knowing Karen and you being sent that email. I know it seems random, but the more I think about it, the less inclined I am to believe that one thing isn't connected to another."

"So you think that someone brought me here? Why would anyone do that?"

Colt hung his jacket over the back of a chair. "I'm not saying that is definitely what happened, but I would like to take a look at the email if you can find it. Just to be sure."

I poured Colt a cup of coffee, then set it on the table. "Okay. I'll look for it. But I'm not even sure I saved it." I took the plate of food we'd left warming out of the oven and set it on the table, then took out a second plate with the salads and set that one next to the hot one. "If you do find reason to suspect that something is going on, please don't mention it to anyone until we can look into it a bit. If I know Georgia, Nikki, Velma, and Lacy, they'll worry, and at this point I have to believe there is nothing for them to be concerned about. I'm quite certain that I wasn't 'brought here.' I needed a change, saw an email that appealed to me, and took a chance on a new start."

Colt picked up a rib and took a bite. "I hope that is what we find, but doing what I do, I can't help but find patterns in random events."

I realized that I tended to do the same thing. I felt a tightening in my stomach, then pushed it away. Holiday Bay was my second chance at life, and I wasn't going to let some coincidence ruin it for me. I knew in my heart that Holiday Bay hadn't chosen me as much as I had chosen Holiday Bay, but more than anything else, I knew that Holiday Bay and I were meant to share a life together. It was here, in my little cottage by the sea, that my soul would heal and my heart would find a way to open itself to love again.

Up Next From Kathi Daley Books

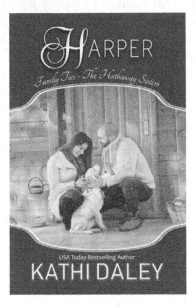

Preview:

Harper Hathaway glanced at the San Francisco skyline as it faded into the distance with the conviction that of all the Hathaway sisters, she was going to go down in family history as having made the biggest mess of her life. Not that making a mess of her life had been what she'd set out to do fourteen years ago, when she'd fled her hometown of

Moosehead, Minnesota, feeling lost and alone in a sea of family and friends. She'd recently graduated high school and had been expected to come up with a plan as to what to do with her life, which at the time seemed pretty overwhelming. Despite a family who loved her, a boyfriend who wanted to marry her, and a grade point average that would have landed her a spot in almost any college in the country, she'd had absolutely no idea who or what she wanted to be. So, after weeks of sleepless nights and angst-filled days, she'd hitched her wagon to the first opportunity she stumbled upon and joined the Army after a recruiter made a cold call to a young woman who actually *was* looking for a life of meaningful adventure in addition to a career.

Looking back, things had worked out all right. At least for a time. Yes, she'd missed her family, and those first years overseas were some of the hardest she'd ever known, but she seemed to have a skill set and personality type that fit well with the lifestyle presented to her, and she'd risen through the ranks at a speed that at times had left her downright dizzy. When time came to re-up after her first tour, she hadn't even considered other options and happily signed on the dotted line. By the time her second contract was complete she was on the fast track to a career with Special Forces, but by the time she'd completed her third contract, she'd seen enough death and destruction to last her a lifetime. She knew in her heart she was ready to try something different and had considered going home to Moosehead, but then she met Eric Palmer, a scuba-diving instructor with a taste for treasure hunting, a bit of wanderlust, and big dreams for the future. Deciding to follow the man and his passion, she moved to San Diego, became a certified scuba diver herself, and followed Eric from one exotic locale to the next. Not only had they traveled the world in search of the ultimate dive site but they'd joined salvage operations along the way. For a brief period in time, she'd really had it all: an exciting life that challenged her both physically and intellectually, a fiancé on the same life path that she had grown to love, and a bright future limited only by what she could imagine. Then, six months ago, her perfect world came tumbling down when her fiancé was killed while diving on a wreck in Cozumel and she'd lost her will to continue down the path they'd chosen to walk together. So one hundred and sixty nine months, two weeks, and eight days after she'd left her home in pursuit of a new life, she found herself returning to Minnesota the same lost and lonely mess she was on the day she'd left.

As she veered from the freeway onto the narrow coastal highway that would take her north, she felt her mood lighten. As a teen, she'd felt stifled in such a small town, but now that her life was such a mess, she realized that after fourteen years out in the world, a large farm perched on a private lake seemed like the optimal place to regroup and heal. As she navigated the narrow, winding road that hugged the rocky shoreline, she tried not to think about what she had lost. She knew in her heart if she was going to ever be able to move forward she had to find a way to stop looking back at what might have been.

After she had driven for several hours, the open coastline gave way to the dense forest of the redwoods. Without the crashing waves to set the mood, her mind began to wander and the fatigue she had been holding at bay began to creep into her consciousness. Deciding that what she really needed was a diversion, she reached forward to switch on the radio. She was momentarily distracted as she searched for a station, which was probably why she hadn't seen the dog that darted onto the road until a split second before it ran in front of her. She slammed on her breaks and turned the wheel hard to the left. She somehow managed to guide the vehicle to a stop, but not before she lost control of it and slid into a drainage ditch that bordered the road. Her heart was pounding a mile a minute by the time she came to a full stop.

"Oh God." She put her hand over her chest. She wasn't hurt, and while the car was going to need to be towed, she didn't think it was badly damaged. She put her hand on the latch and opened the driver's side door. Taking a deep breath to steady shaky knees, she slowly climbed out. She was pretty sure she was fine, but the dog… Oh God, the dog. She looked around the area and didn't see a dog, injured or otherwise. She didn't think she'd hit him. She slowly made her way up the embankment and looked around. She couldn't see the dog, but after a moment she heard him whimpering from the other side of the road. The sun had set and the sky was beginning to grow dim, so she pulled on her jacket, grabbed the flashlight she kept for emergencies, and jogged across the road. "Are you okay?"

The yellow Labrador, which was really no more than a puppy, continued to whine, so she walked slowly forward. "I won't hurt you," she said in a soft voice. "I just want to help." The pup didn't move, and he didn't attack either, so she took a few more steps.

Not only had she grown up on a farm but her mother was a veterinarian. She'd lived around animals her entire life and generally knew how to calm them. She could see that this one was scared, but he also seemed to want her to help.

"I'm going to come closer," she said in a soft voice.

The dog watched her warily but didn't move toward her. When she was within a few feet of him, he moved away. She took a few more steps. He moved a few of his own. She supposed at some point he must have realized that she was going to continue to follow because he limped down the embankment and into the dense forest. He hadn't gone far when she noticed something blue. A car. The dog had led her to a car that must have veered off the road. There was still steam coming from its engine compartment, so she had to assume the accident had recently occurred.

She made her way toward the car as fast as the steep terrain would allow, slipping only once on the muddy ground. When she reached the car, she headed directly to the open driver's side door and looked inside. There was a man in the seat who was still buckled in with a large gash on his head. He appeared to be unconscious. She looked into the interior of the vehicle and found a woman in the passenger seat. She likewise appeared to be unconscious. Taking a quick peek into the rear of the vehicle, she saw a baby strapped into a car seat.

"A baby," she said a little too loudly. She must have startled the dog because he began to bark aggressively. "It's okay," she said in a gentler voice.

"I'm going to go around to the back and open the door so I can see what needs to be done. Okay?"

The dog stopped barking but didn't move from the position he had taken up near the open driver's side door. When she arrived at the back door, Harper assured the dog once again that he could trust her. She opened the door and gently ran her hands over the baby, who was awake and appeared to be unharmed. She unstrapped the car seat, lifted the baby out, and cradled the whimpering infant it in her arms. "It's okay. I have you now. It's okay. I'm going to get help."

She walked back around to the front of the vehicle to check on the driver. She felt for a pulse, and he opened his eyes. "The baby," he gasped. "You need to hide the baby."

"Hide the baby?"

"Hurry. You must leave now. Don't trust anyone."

She froze in indecision. The man had lost a lot of blood. She had to wonder if he was delirious. She looked toward the woman in the passenger seat. "The baby's mother?"

The man nodded. "Dead. Now hurry. Take the diaper bag. It is up to you to keep the baby safe."

She looked down at the infant in her arms. He or she appeared to have drifted off. She didn't feel right about leaving the man and woman in the car and was trying to make up her mind about the options available to her when she heard another car on the road. She wasn't sure why she made the decision to hide. Instinct, she supposed. One minute she was contemplating the idea of calling 911 and the next she was heading toward the cover of the trees with the baby cradled snuggly in her arms and the long handle of the diaper bag draped over her shoulder. The puppy, who seemed to have settled down now that she had the baby, trailed along behind her.

After a few minutes of searching for an adequate hiding place, she found an outcropping of rocks that, combined with the darkening sky, seemed to provide a sufficient amount of cover. She tightened one arm around the baby, caressed the puppy with the other, crouched down as low as she could manage, and watched as a man in a highway patrol uniform hiked down the embankment, walked over to the car, said something to the driver, took out a gun, and shot him. The pup began to growl. She shushed him and then watched as the patrolman walked around the vehicle and shot the woman in the passenger seat, although, according to the driver of the vehicle, she was already dead. The accident hadn't appeared to have been serious enough to be responsible for the woman's death, so Harper had to assume she had died before that, from an injury or illness. After he shot the woman in the passenger seat, the officer opened the back door and stuck his head inside. She held her breath when she realized that he must be looking for the baby. After rooting around in the rear of the vehicle for a moment, he took several steps away from it and looked around.

Her heart pounded as she continued to crouch behind the rocks, calming the puppy and whispering to the baby. It was a cold day in February and the blanket in which someone had wrapped the baby wasn't all that heavy, so Harper unzipped her jacket, slipped the baby inside, and then scrunched down even smaller and waited. The puppy climbed into her lap, providing an extra layer of warmth for the baby as the man in the uniform continued to search the immediate area. The tall, thin man, with dark hair and a crooked nose, took several steps in her direction, pausing only a few yards from the rocks where she was hiding. If not for her military training, she was certain she would have screamed or fainted or both. The baby let out a tiny cry, so she tightened her arms around the bundle she'd nestled to her chest and prayed the puppy would remain quiet and the baby would go back to sleep.

After a few minutes, the man headed back toward the vehicle for a second look, opened both the trunk and the engine compartment, rooted around, circled back toward them, and then pulled out his phone and spoke in a deep voice. "Agent Beaverton is dead, as is the witness. The baby is gone and there is no sign of the ledger. There is a car in the ditch just off the road. I assume that its driver found our target and went for help. I'm going to see if there is ID inside the vehicle. The driver can't have gotten far."

Harper watched as the man turned and headed back toward the road. After he'd driven away, she scooted out from behind the rocks and let out a long breath of relief before the puppy, the baby, and she slowly made their way back toward her car. It was almost completely dark now, and getting colder by the minute. She knew she needed to get help, but her car was disabled, and a quick search of her vehicle confirmed that the man who had shot the occupants of the vehicle carrying the baby had taken her purse and her phone, as well as her vehicle registration.

"Okay, this can't be good," she mumbled. She supposed it made sense to stay with the vehicle.

Someone would come along eventually. Of course, the man who had been with the baby had said not to trust anyone, and it had been a man in a highway patrolman's uniform who had shot and killed him in cold blood. Maybe waiting with the car wasn't the best idea. She'd been heading toward a small town she knew was just north of her position when the accident occurred. The town was still quite a ways off, but she'd driven this road before, and she seemed to remember a rundown little motel connected to a gas station and a small eatery not all that far up the road. Staying in a motel so close to the spot where her car had been disabled might not be the smartest thing to do given the fact that there was at least one man she knew of looking for the baby she'd tucked beneath her jacket. Still, staying with the car was probably the worst thing she could do, so she began to walk along the side of the road with the baby in her arms and the puppy trailing along beside her. The baby hadn't been very active since she'd plucked it from its car seat. This, she had to admit, worried her. Had it been hurt in the accident despite the lack of blood? He or she had been strapped into a high-quality infant car carrier that appeared to have shielded the tiny thing from the worst of the impact, but she supposed the infant could have sustained internal injuries. She didn't have a lot of options at this point, so she hiked the diaper bag more firmly over her shoulder and continued to walk, praying all the while that a solution to her dilemma would present itself before it was too late.

"'Closed for the season.'" She groaned as she read the sign nailed to the front the motel, gas station, and eatery she'd remembered. It had taken her forty minutes of steady walking to arrive here, and she couldn't remember there being another town for a good twenty to thirty miles more. She needed to get the baby inside and out of the cold, so, making a quick decision, she made her way over to the small motel and used the multiuse knife she always kept in her pocket to break into one of the rooms farthest away from the road. Once the puppy, the baby, and she were inside, she tried the lights, but the electricity was turned off. She used the flashlight she still had in her pocket to provide at least a modicum of light. She unzipped her jacket, removed the bundled-up baby, and laid it on the bed. The puppy jumped up onto the bed and stretched out next to it.

"Hey, sweetie, how are you doing?" she cooed to the child.

The baby opened its eyes.

"I know that you are probably wet and hungry. Hopefully, there will be supplies in the bag that will take care of both those problems."

She slid the diaper bag off her shoulder and emptied its contents onto the bed. A package of diapers, baby wipes, a can of powdered formula, several bottles of purified water, a couple of pairs of warm pajamas, and a thumb drive. Everything made sense except the thumb drive. She slipped the drive into her pocket and unwrapped the baby from the blanket. She took off the wet diaper to find that her traveling companion was a little girl. She quickly changed the baby's diaper, then dressed her in the warmest pajamas she could find. Once she was clean and dry, she wrapped her in the blanket she'd found her in, then pulled the blanket from the bed over her as well. Harper had no way of knowing when the baby had last been fed, but her tiny little whimper seemed like a *feed me* sort of cry, so she read the instructions on the can of formula, mixed up a bottle, and then held it to the baby's lips. She took a single suck, then began to cry. The bottle was ice cold, and having had three younger sisters, Harper could remember that babies liked to have their bottles warmed. She made sure the baby was tucked securely on the bed, then went into the bathroom, praying for hot water. Just because the electricity was off didn't mean the gas was off as well.

She held her breath as she turned on the faucet. The water was ice cold at first, but after a moment it began to warm up. She filled the basin with hot water, then held the bottle in it until the formula felt warmer. She made her way back to the bed, arranged the pillows against the headboard, and leaned into them as she cradled the baby in her arms. Thankfully, she devoured the bottle as the puppy snuggled in next to them and fell fast asleep.

"So, what on earth have you gotten yourself in to?" she asked the tiny baby as she sucked the bottle. "You seem a little young to have made enemies, yet there apparently are some really bad people after you." She remembered the man in the uniform. "Or at least one really bad man." She wondered if the man who shot the accident survivor was a dirty cop, or if he was an assassin who had stolen a uniform. The man who had been traveling with the baby had told her not to trust anyone, which led her to believe that he knew that whoever was after the baby had connections in high places.

Once the baby fell asleep, she tucked her under the covers and then got up and took a look around the room. She needed a plan that included something other than just sitting around waiting for the man to find them. She wasn't even sure it was safe to stay in the room until morning, although taking the baby out into the chilly night air wasn't an option either, so she supposed her best bet was to hunker down and wait for sunrise. The question was, what then?

She didn't have her phone, ID, wallet, credit or bank card. The man in the car had said to trust no one, but she did have people in her life she knew she could trust. Her mother, grandmother, and three sisters would all help her in a minute, but she didn't want to drag any of them into whatever was going on until she figured out exactly *what* was going on. The man in the CHP uniform had taken her registration, but the address on it was that of her apartment in San Diego. Still, the man had her name, and she was afraid that once he figured out who she was, he would be able to backtrack and find her family in Minnesota, so perhaps she should warn them. The problem was that she didn't know how to warn them without worrying them.

She paced around the room as she tried to work out her options. Thinking of her family made her think of her hometown, Moosehead, and there was one person there she could trust who would have the skill set necessary to do whatever he had to in this situation. Ben Holiday was a private investigator and an ex-cop. He had moved to Moosehead after she had moved away and was married to an old high-school friend of hers, Holly Thompson. Or at least she had been Holly Thompson before she married the handsome PI, opened a foster care home, and built a family. Harper had met Ben three years ago, while she was living in San Diego. He'd been hired to track down a missing teenager who'd last been seen near Coronado Island. Holly knew that she lived in the area and suggested that Ben contact her for help with the search. In the end, she had helped him track down the missing teen and, in the process, made a lifelong friend.

The more Harper thought about it, the more she realized that contacting Ben was her best bet. Now she just needed to figure out how to get in touch with him without a phone. A quick search of the room confirmed that there wasn't one in it, but maybe the office? The electricity had been off, but the gas had been left on, so perhaps the phone had been left on as well. It would make sense the phone would remain in service so that anyone who called the motel unaware that it was closed for the season could leave a message on an answering machine, which, she bet, was the sort of messaging system this old motel would use.

She walked over to the bed to check on the baby, who was still asleep next to the puppy. Making a quick decision, she grabbed her pocket knife and flashlight and then headed out into the cold night air. The motel office was just off the highway, so she knew she'd need to be careful not to be seen, but while this area was popular with hikers and campers during the summer, the place would be all but deserted on a cold night in February.

She had just left the shelter of the room at the back of the lot and had started across the pavement when a set of headlights appeared from the south. She quickly ducked behind a large redwood, where she waited until the car drove by. When it had passed, she continued toward the office and café. She was just passing the gas pumps when another set of headlights appeared on the horizon. Apparently, she'd been wrong about the place being deserted. She ducked behind one of the pumps and watched as a CHP vehicle slowed and then pulled into the lot. She froze as the car stopped in front of the motel office. A tall man got out and walked over to the door. It wasn't the same one she had seen shoot the two car accident victims, but not knowing who to trust, she stayed put. The man knocked on the door, then tried the lock. He shone his flashlight around, missing her hiding spot by inches. He walked back to the car and then pulled out a handheld radio. "Redwood Junction is clear. The place is locked up tight and there is no sign of the driver of the vehicle or the baby. I'll continue to keep my eyes open. They can't have gotten far unless the driver managed to hitch a ride."

He took one last look around, got into his car, and drove away. She let out the breath she'd been holding since he pulled into the lot. She figured she was safe for now, but come daylight, it would be a different story altogether. After making sure there were no other headlights in either direction, she ran to the front door of the motel office. She quickly picked the lock and slipped inside. She knew she couldn't risk a light, even the one from the flashlight, so she felt around until she found the desk where she suspected she'd find the phone. She let out a long sigh of relief when she got a dial tone. She momentarily wondered whether using the phone might somehow give away her location, but right now she needed a way out of this mess, so she took a chance and dialed the familiar number.

She listened as the line was answered by a recording. "You have reached Holiday Investigations. We are currently unavailable or on another line, but if you leave your name and number, someone will call you back."

"Ben, this is Harper Hathaway. I need help. Don't call my cell or text or try to reach me using any of my known contact information. I'm going to try your cell. If that doesn't work, I'll try back in a half hour."

She hung up and then dialed Ben's cell.

"Harper, I just got your message. I was hoping you'd try the cell. What's going on?"

She explained about the accident, the baby, the warning issued by the man in the car, and the uniformed officer who had shot him.

"Wow." Ben paused. "I'm not sure what to say. I can't imagine what is going on that would cause a highway patrolman to shoot a man and a woman in cold blood."

"There was a thumb drive in the diaper bag that might explain what is going on, but I don't have a way to read it. I'm not sure what to do. I don't have transportation, ID, or money, and the man who was driving the car with the baby said not to trust anyone. After seeing a man in uniform shoot him and the woman with him and the baby with my own eyes, I'm hesitant to call 9-1-1. I don't think that staying here is an option. The highway patrol seem to be checking on the place. It is cold and damp and I am traveling with a puppy and an infant. I need help and I need it fast."

Ben paused for a moment before replying. "I have a friend, Michael Maddox. He is a tech whiz and we have worked together on a few cases. He is actually in California this month, setting up a security system for a financial planning firm. I'm going to give him a call. If he is still in the same location he was when I last spoke to him, he should be able to get to you in five or six hours."

She let out a sigh of relief. "That would be great."

"Since I can't call you, how about you call me back in thirty minutes?"

******

Michael Maddox pulled into the lot at his hotel. He'd been in California for a month now and was beginning to feel the tug in his chest calling him home. Not that he really minded that his job as a cyber security consultant and software developer took him all over the world, but after this long on the road, he always felt the urge to head back to Minnesota. Today was his last day on this particular job, so it wouldn't be long before he would be able to leave the temperate climate of Central California for the subzero temperatures in the north.

With the completion of this job, he would basically be unemployed for the next six weeks. He was sure he could rustle something up if he really wanted to work, but it had been a while since he'd had time to relax. Maybe he'd take some time off to enjoy the rest of the winter. It had been eons since he'd gone ice fishing. Maybe he'd call his friend, Ben Holiday. It had been forever since the two of them had taken a guys' trip. Of course, Michael acknowledged, Ben was a busy man. Not only was he married to a popular advice columnist who traveled for work almost as often as he did, but the couple had built a blended family consisting of biological, adopted, and foster children that appeared to keep him on his toes.

He turned off the ignition and was beginning to gather his belongings when his phone rang. He answered without bothering to check his caller ID. "Maddox here."

"Michael, its Megan."

Michael smiled at the sound of his middle sister's voice. "Meg, how are you?"

"Busy. I only have a minute, but I wanted to call to make sure you've made your travel reservations."

"Travel reservations?"

"Mom and Dad's anniversary. You do remember? You promised."

He did remember, although for the life of him, he'd been trying to forget. "I know I promised, but I'm in California on a job. It's taking longer than I anticipated. I don't think I'm going to make it back in time."

"Not making it back is not an option," Megan insisted in a stern voice. "Neither Macy nor Marley are going to make it back, which means that it is up to you and me."

Michael winced. He felt bad about missing his parents' anniversary party yet again, but he really, really didn't want to go home.

"Please, Michael." He couldn't help but hear the desperation in her voice. "I'm counting on you to be there."

"You know how busy I am," Michael tried.

"Really?" He could hear the desperation turn to anger. "You are going to use the *I'm busy* excuse with your younger sister, who is not only doing a demanding surgical rotation as part of her pediatric residency at one of the most demanding hospitals in the country but is applying for jobs at every major hospital in the world and is planning the entire party by herself?"

Michael groaned. She had him there. "Okay. I'm sorry. I'll be home. I promise. Will it just be you and me and Mom and Dad?"

"No. Matthew and Julia will be there as well."

Michael didn't reply. Despite Megan's efforts to keep the family together, it seemed as if there had been one obstacle after another. First there was Maddie, and then there was Julia. Totally different situations, but family dividers all the same.

"I know that Matthew attending the party is the real reason you don't want to come," Megan continued. "And I know you have a good reason to want to avoid him, but this isn't about you. It is about finding a way to be a family despite our challenges, and the parents who sacrificed a lot while we were growing up so that we could follow our dreams as adults."

Michael hung his head. "I know. I'm sorry. I'll make the reservations tonight. I'll call you later with the details."

"Thanks," Megan sighed in relief. "I know this is difficult for you."

"It's not difficult," Michael lied. "In fact, I'm totally over it. So, how is the job hunt going?" He wanted desperately to move the subject away from his twin brother and ex-fiancée.

"Slowly. I am more than qualified for every job I have applied for. And I have excellent references. The problem is, the other applicants who have applied for those same jobs are equally qualified. Maybe even more qualified. I have to admit that I am beginning to become discouraged. I really hoped to have a job to go to when my residency was finished in May."

"It sounds tough, but I know the perfect job is waiting for you. Maybe you just haven't stumbled across it."

"I love your optimism, but I don't think my lack of 'stumbling' is the reason I haven't even been granted an interview." Meg groaned. "Perhaps I should lower my standards. I really thought I would be able to snag one of the elite jobs I've always dreamed of, but elite jobs attract elite candidates, and there are a lot more of them than I ever imagined."

"Hang in there, sis. The perfect job is out there."

"Easy for you to say. You've somehow managed to do a wonderful job of stumbling your way through life without so much as the beginnings of a plan. I, on the other hand, have adhered to a rigid set of goals and objectives since I was a teenager, and where has it gotten me?"

"A residency at one of the best hospitals in the country."

Meg laughed. "I guess you are right. Enough with the whining. I'm really looking forward to seeing you. We all are."

"And I'm looking forward to seeing you as well." Michael looked at the screen when his cell beeped. "Listen, I have to go. Ben Holiday is on the other line."

"You'll make the reservations? Tonight?"

"I will. I promise."

"Don't let me down, big bro. I'm counting on you."

"I'll be there with bells on. Love you."

"Love you too."

Michael hung up with Megan and answered Ben's call. "I was just thinking about you."

"You were?"

Michael glanced at the first drops of rain as they landed on his windshield. "I've finished up here and am planning to head home in the next day or two. Are you up for some ice fishing?"

"I am. But first I need a favor. A big favor."

******

Harper headed back to check on the baby while she waited. She let herself out of the office door, locked it behind her just in case, then paused, considering the small café. It was closed for the season, but they may have left something behind. If nothing else, she wanted to find something for the puppy. She pulled out her knife, picked one more lock, and slipped inside. She headed to the kitchen to find that the cabinets were bare with the exception of a few canned items. When she came across a can of SPAM, she figured that would work for the puppy, so she grabbed it, along with a can of peaches, then slipped out of the café, locked the door, and sprinted across the dark lot toward the room where she'd left the sleeping dog and infant.

"I have food," she said to the pup, who raised his head and wagged his tail when she came in. The baby was still sleeping peacefully, so she used her knife to open both the SPAM and the peaches. The pup inhaled the food without even stopping to chew and then jumped back onto the bed, curled up with the baby, and went back to sleep. She plucked one of the peaches from the heavy syrup and nibbled on it, but her appetite was pretty much nonexistent, so she set the can aside. She wasn't sure what she was going to do if Ben's friend was no longer in the area, or if he was unable to help her for some reason. Both her experience in the Army and her life as a scuba diver and treasure hunter had taught her to think on her feet no matter the situation. And she was good at doing just that, in most cases. But in most cases she didn't have a baby and a puppy to think about.

She drew the curtains closed except for a small sliver she could peek through. Shutting out the natural light provided by the moon made the room even darker, but she had no way of knowing if the patrolman who had been by earlier would come back again and she wasn't taking any chances. She knew that it was vital to any good plan to have an escape route. She'd chosen the room on the end, which had a small window in the bathroom the others didn't appear to have. It would be a tight squeeze to get herself, the baby, and the puppy through the narrow opening, but if push came to shove, that was exactly what she would do.

She took the thumb drive out of her pocket and looked at it. She didn't have her computer or any other way to read it, but she felt it might be the key to what had been going on with the people in the car. There was an ancient computer in the office, but without electricity to run it, it did her little good.

She froze as a car pulled into the lot. She crossed the room and peeked out the window. It was a dark-colored minivan. Chances were it belonged to a passing motorist who'd remembered the small travel stop and hoped to find gas or lodging. The van sat in the lot for two or three minutes before continuing on.

Harper didn't have her phone or a watch, so she had no way to keep track of time, but after she assumed thirty minutes could have passed, she checked on the baby and the puppy, both of whom were still asleep, and let herself out of the room to go back to the office. She picked up the phone and dialed Ben's number.

"Everything is set," he said as soon as he answered. "Michael was just getting back to his hotel when I called. He is going to grab a few things and will be on the road heading in your direction within half an hour. The traffic should be light at this time of night, so he estimates he should reach you in about six hours. He won't be able to call you, but I am going to give you his cell number so you can check in with him if you'd like."

"Okay, great." She rooted around for a pen and paper and took down the number.

"It's nine o'clock now, so look for him at around three."

"What make, model, and color car will he be driving?"

"Black Range Rover with Minnesota plates."

"Okay, I'll look for him. And thanks, Ben. I don't know what I would do if you couldn't help. I'm usually pretty good at taking care of myself, but with an infant and a puppy, I'm afraid I'm a bit out of my depth."

"How is the baby?"

"She seems okay, which is amazing because she can't be more than a few days old and was just involved in a serious accident. The car seat she was strapped into was a good one, and the car didn't look as if it had rolled, which may be why she appears to be unharmed."

"Is she eating?"

"She is. She is not a fan of a cold bottle, but the gas is still on, so I used hot tap water to warm it."

She listened as Ben let out a breath. "That's good. I'll feel better once Michael gets there. He is a good guy and you can trust him. The fact that a CHP officer seems to be involved in whatever is going on has me worried, but I guess we'll just take things one challenge at a time until we can work things through."

"It will be fine," she said, even though she didn't necessarily believe it. "I should get back to the room to check on the baby."

"Before you go, I want you to describe the highway patrolman you saw shoot the occupants of the vehicle. I'm going to see if I can track down his identity."

"Tall. Over six feet. Short dark hair. Thin. Crooked nose, which looked to have been broken in the past." Harper paused and thought about him. "I didn't get a real close look so I can't tell you his eye color. I guess the crooked nose is the best clue I can provide."

"Okay. I'll see what I can find out. Be careful and check in when you can."

She rang off, then slipped out of the office and went back to the room where she'd left the baby and puppy. The puppy looked as if he wanted to go out, so she took a quick peek at the baby, who was still sleeping, and took him out behind the building in case a car came down the road. She really, really hoped that the highway patrol wouldn't be back, but she had no way of knowing when or if they would.

The puppy did his thing and she took him back to the room, then tried to get some rest. She fed and changed the baby again at around eleven o'clock. After the baby settled down and went back to sleep, she took the puppy out one more time, then laid down beside both of them. She'd tucked the baby in next to her chest, and the puppy settled on her other side. She was sure the baby would be warm despite the fact that the room was not heated. She must have fallen asleep at some point, although she'd intended to stay awake. When she noticed headlights shining in through the window, she assumed it was Michael Maddox. She got up and peeked out of the small opening in the curtain and almost had a heart attack when she saw it was a CHP vehicle. She could only hope whoever had stopped by would take a quick look around and drive on.

She kept the drapes drawn, so other than the small crack visible between them, she couldn't see much. She looked at the pup, who had started to growl. "Don't bark." She ordered, then glanced at the bathroom behind her. The baby was still asleep, but if the pup barked, he would give them away for sure. She gently picked up the baby, grabbed the diaper bag, called softly to the puppy, and moved everyone to the bathroom. She closed the door except for a narrow crack she could peek through. She could hear whoever had gotten out of the car knocking on and then jiggling the handle of every door. Had she locked the room door the last time she took the puppy out?

She heard the knock on their door and waited for the jiggle before she heard another car pull up. The man who had been checking doors seemed to have walked away because she heard him greet whoever had just arrived. She couldn't hear what was being said, but after a few minutes, she heard both vehicles drive away. She waited where she was for several minutes, then slowly opened the bathroom door. She hadn't heard anything since the vehicles had pulled away and was about to sneak over to the window for a quick look when the door opened to reveal a tall, broad-shouldered man carrying a gun.

Apple Pie Biscuits

Preheat oven to 375 degrees.

Spray a 6 x 9 baking dish on all sides with nonstick spray.

Open 1 can large buttermilk biscuits (I use Pillsbury Grands).

Melt 1 stick (½ cup) butter (I melt it in a bowl in the microwave).

Combine in a bowl:
½ cup white sugar
½ cup brown sugar
1 tsp. nutmeg
1 tbs. cinnamon

Prepare biscuits:
Dip each one into butter, coating on both sides, then dip into sugar mixture, coating on both sides. Place into baking dish.

The topping:
Top with one can of apple pie filling.

Combine remaining butter with remaining sugar mixture. Add ½ cup oatmeal and 1 cup chopped pecans. Pour over top of biscuits.

Bake at 375 degrees for 35 minutes.

Drizzle over top when baked:

Combine
1 cup powdered sugar
¼ cup heavy cream

Serve hot.

Books by Kathi Daley

Come for the murder, stay for the romance.

Zoe Donovan Cozy Mystery:

Halloween Hijinks
The Trouble With Turkeys
Christmas Crazy
Cupid's Curse
Big Bunny Bump-off
Beach Blanket Barbie
Maui Madness
Derby Divas
Haunted Hamlet
Turkeys, Tuxes, and Tabbies
Christmas Cozy
Alaskan Alliance
Matrimony Meltdown
Soul Surrender
Heavenly Honeymoon
Hopscotch Homicide
Ghostly Graveyard
Santa Sleuth
Shamrock Shenanigans
Kitten Kaboodle
Costume Catastrophe
Candy Cane Caper
Holiday Hangover
Easter Escapade
Camp Carter

Trick or Treason
Reindeer Roundup
Hippity Hoppity Homicide
Firework Fiasco
Henderson House
Holiday Hostage
Lunacy Lake – *Summer 2019*

Zimmerman Academy The New Normal
Zimmerman Academy New Beginnings
Ashton Falls Cozy Cookbook

Tj Jensen Paradise Lake Mysteries by Henery Press:

Pumpkins in Paradise
Snowmen in Paradise
Bikinis in Paradise
Christmas in Paradise
Puppies in Paradise
Halloween in Paradise
Treasure in Paradise
Fireworks in Paradise
Beaches in Paradise
Thanksgiving in Paradise – *Fall 2019*

Whales and Tails Cozy Mystery:

Romeow and Juliet
The Mad Catter
Grimm's Furry Tail

Much Ado About Felines
Legend of Tabby Hollow
Cat of Christmas Past
A Tale of Two Tabbies
The Great Catsby
Count Catula
The Cat of Christmas Present
A Winter's Tail
The Taming of the Tabby
Frankencat
The Cat of Christmas Future
Farewell to Felines
A Whisker in Time
The Catsgiving Feast
A Whale of a Tail – *Spring 2019*

Writers' Retreat Southern Seashore Mystery:

First Case
Second Look
Third Strike
Fourth Victim
Fifth Night
Sixth Cabin
Seventh Chapter
Eighth Witness

Rescue Alaska Paranormal Mystery:

Finding Justice

Finding Answers
Finding Courage
Finding Christmas
Finding Shelter – *Spring 2019*

A Tess and Tilly Mystery:

The Christmas Letter
The Valentine Mystery
The Mother's Day Mishap
The Halloween House
The Thanksgiving Trip
The Saint Paddy's Promise – *March 2019*

The Inn at Holiday Bay:

Boxes in the Basement
Letters in the Library
Message in the Mantel – *Spring 2019*

Family Ties:

The Hathaway Sisters
Harper – *February 2019*
Harlow – *Spring 2019*

Haunting by the Sea:

Homecoming by the Sea
Secrets by the Sea
Missing by the Sea
Betrayal by the Sea – *March 2019*

Sand and Sea Hawaiian Mystery:

Murder at Dolphin Bay
Murder at Sunrise Beach
Murder at the Witching Hour
Murder at Christmas
Murder at Turtle Cove
Murder at Water's Edge
Murder at Midnight

Seacliff High Mystery:

The Secret
The Curse
The Relic
The Conspiracy
The Grudge
The Shadow
The Haunting

Road to Christmas Romance:

Road to Christmas Past

USA Today best-selling author Kathi Daley lives in beautiful Lake Tahoe with her husband Ken. When she isn't writing, she likes spending time hiking the miles of desolate trails surrounding her home. She has authored more than seventy-five books in eight series, including Zoe Donovan Cozy Mysteries, Whales and Tails Island Mysteries, Sand and Sea Hawaiian Mysteries, Tj Jensen Paradise Lake Series, Writers' Retreat Southern Seashore Mysteries, Rescue Alaska Paranormal Mysteries, and Seacliff High Teen Mysteries. Find out more about her books at www.kathidaley.com

Stay up-to-date:

Newsletter, *The Daley Weekly*
http://eepurl.com/NRPDf
Webpage – www.kathidaley.com
Facebook at Kathi Daley Books –
www.facebook.com/kathidaleybooks
Kathi Daley Books Group Page –
https://www.facebook.com/groups/569578823146850/
E-mail – kathidaley@kathidaley.com
Twitter at Kathi Daley@kathidaley –
https://twitter.com/kathidaley
Amazon Author Page –
https://www.amazon.com/author/kathidaley
BookBub –
https://www.bookbub.com/authors/kathi-daley